"A perfect read on every level"

SEAN

"Whenever I'm feeling down, or stressed, or worried about exams, I can lose myself in an adventure with the COLAs"

EMILY

"I feel as if I am actually inside the story"

MORGAN

"It's been my favourite series for so many years now"

IOANA

"Thank you . . . for writing something that's helped me so much over the years"

ADELAIDE

WELCOME TO THE SHAPESHIFTER UNIVERSE

- - -

A NOTE FROM THE AUTHOR

When Dax Jones first showed up in my head, skinny, dark-eyed and restless, I had no idea how much he was going to mean to me. As a journalist I interviewed a lot of celebrities. They were fun—but the best stories I ever got were not from celebs. They came from normal people whose lives had been suddenly changed in some unexpected way. They were the *real* deal.

So Dax showed up kind of ordinary. And yet not. His name is a clue. Half ordinary, half extraordinary. I wanted to write about supernatural stuff but not in a wifty-wafty way. I wanted to imagine it as I believe it really would be. So I played the 'what if' game. What if you changed shape one day? Just shifted into something else? In this world—here, today. *Right now* while you're reading this. Look around you. How would people react if you were suddenly holding this page open with the claws and snout of a fox?

Ready to find out? Just sit back and enjoy the ride . . .

For Simon, Jacob, and Alex

OXFORD
UNIVERSITY PRESS

Great Clarendon Street, Oxford OX2 6DP
Oxford University Press is a department of the University of Oxford.
It furthers the University's objective of excellence in research, scholarship,
and education by publishing worldwide. Oxford is a registered trade mark of
Oxford University Press in the UK and in certain other countries

Copyright © Ali Sparkes 2006
The moral rights of the author have been asserted
Database right Oxford University Press (maker)
First published 2006
First published in this edition 2016

British Library Cataloguing in Publication Data
Data available
ISBN: 978-0-19-275983-2

1 3 5 7 9 10 8 6 4 2
Printed and bound in India by Replika Press Pvt. Ltd.
Paper used in the production of this book is a natural,
recyclable product made from wood grown in sustainable forests.
The manufacturing process conforms to the environmental
regulations of the country of origin.

THE SHAPESHIFTER

FINDING THE FOX

ALI SPARKES

OXFORD
UNIVERSITY PRESS

BEFORE

A dark shape came to him in the soft grey mist of not quite awake and not quite asleep. It moved around the small strip of floor next to his bed but didn't frighten him, exactly. The way it breathed and the way its clawed feet snagged hesitantly on the thin carpet told him it was sad. That it had known great pain.

And it was leaving.

1

Dax Jones spent a lot of time in the back garden. Thinking about his attitude.

It was an unlovely garden; a rectangle of uneven grass with charmless grey-green bushes at its edge, split by a concrete path which led to the shed, behind which was a compost heap. A washing line stretched between two posts almost the entire length of it, kinked by pegs and sagging in the middle.

Today the back door was banged shut so hard the panes rattled. Through the glass Dax could see Gina shooting the top and bottom bolts across, the undersides of her pudgy upper arms swinging violently with the effort. 'You can do some weeding while you're out there,' she said, her voice muted by the glass, but still sharp with dislike. Dax hadn't had the right expression on his face during lunch. Even though he ate all the burnt bits without complaint, his attitude had sneaked up on him, apparently. Again.

'Alice and I are going to town and when we get back I'll expect to see the garden weed-free. We won't be back till teatime, so if you need a drink you can use the outside tap.'

She regarded him through the glass for a moment.

Dax tried to remain still and expressionless. 'And you can take that stuck-up look off your face!' she suddenly snapped, and then turned on her heel and was gone.

Dax let out a sigh of relief and sank down onto one of the white plastic patio chairs on the four feet of concrete outside the patio doors. The mildewy water lying in its lowest curve immediately seeped into the seat of his jeans. Dax stood up again. He was perfectly still and perfectly quiet. At the front of the house he heard the door open and slam shut, Alice's shrill voice from the drive, Gina's reply, keys jingling and, finally, the car departing.

In the silence that followed, anyone watching the boy in the back garden might have thought he was calm. Meditating, even. And it was true that Dax often *seemed* calm.

Dax never shouted. Dax barely even raised his voice at home. It wasn't that he didn't get angry. He sometimes got so angry he could explode. There had been times when he'd been so angry he'd frightened even himself, like the summer evening when Gina had cleared out all his wildlife books and art stuff, and given them to a jumble sale collector. 'When you've got your *own* house you can fill it with junk,' she'd said to him, hands on her hips on the upstairs landing, *daring* him to argue. He'd been so filled with fury and bitterness that he'd nearly—truly, *honestly*—run at her and pushed her down the stairs. He had actually *seen* himself do it, *felt* the warm gasp of air from her shocked mouth in the millisecond before he shoved, heard her shrieks of rage and the noisy, satisfying thuds as she bounced from step to step and hit the hallway floor like a sack of sand.

Only, of course, he hadn't. He'd just screwed up his fists in his pockets and dug his fingernails into his palms so hard that four tiny crescents could still be found in each an hour later. And then he'd gone quietly back into his room to look at the gap under his bed, where his treasured books, paper, and charcoal had once been. It looked back at him, balefully, like an empty eye socket.

Over the years he'd learned a trick. When he started to feel that shake in the pit of his stomach, that feeling like an earthquake under the planet's crust, getting ready to spew blazing molten rock right up and out into space, he pushed down hard with his mind. He pushed down hard with an imaginary thick metal bin-lid and squashed the angry lava back down into his core. In his head he tried to see his lava cooling down and going dull red and then grey and clunky like in those pictures of the lower slopes of Mount Etna. Eventually he'd make it go solid and cold.

The only problem with this was that several volcanoes' worth of cold anger was knocking around inside Dax Jones. He went around with an almost permanent stomach ache. Even he didn't realize how heavy it made him.

He walked the concrete path to the shed to find a hoe for breaking up the weedy patch that ran from the compost heap to the scrubby low brambles at the far end of the garden. When Gina had said 'weed-free' he'd known better than to think she was joking.

The small shed was a warm, woody chamber of old balls of raffia, plastic pots, gardening tools, and bags of peat. Its door was unlocked, but kept from swinging in the wind by a stout piece of wood, which turned a 180 degree arc on a stout nail. It was loose and you had to watch it didn't swing down and clout you on the temple as you walked in. Dax shoved it up, holding it in place as he pulled open the door and wandered into the little shed. He spent a fair bit of time in here on days when he was 'thinking about his attitude'.

He rummaged into the far corner for the hoe, and as he was trying to untangle it from the skinny grip of the rake, there was a sudden gust of wind outside and, with a woody thud, the shed door banged shut. Dax hauled out the hoe with a final tug and had turned to go back outside when there was a tiny squeaking sound and a small clop. It wasn't until he pushed the door that he realized what this meant. The thick wooden latch had just flopped back down. It had often done this, but never in the seconds that followed a sharp north-easterly gust of wind. Never just as the shed door had slammed shut, with a boy inside.

No matter how unlikely this chain of events might seem, Dax realized, with a jolt in his carefully quietened body, that it just *had*. He was shut in. He shoved hard against the door. It didn't budge at all. He gritted his teeth and eyed the small window, but unless he was prepared to smash it, that was no good. It didn't open. There was a loose plank at the back, behind the bags of peat. He pulled the heavy vinyl sacks aside and prodded at it, but there was no way he could fit through the gap.

With a sigh, Dax sank on to the floor of the shed and prepared to wait out the three or four hours until his stepmum and half-sister came back. By now they would probably have arrived at the giant indoor shopping centre on the edge of town, where they would spend an astonishing amount of money on something pink and glittery to go either on some part of Alice, or in some part of her room. A pinker and more doll-filled room than Alice's you couldn't hope to find—but there was always something that could be added to it.

Dax had the smallest bedroom at the darkest end of the house, where a damp patch leached through in the corner under the eaves. The window in it was high up and shallow, like a letterbox. A network of tiny wires ran through the glass, so if you smashed it the pane wouldn't shatter, but just hang there like a crunched-up clear mint. The mean amount of light that filtered in through it came only for a couple of hours at the end of the day. The room was just big enough for his bed and a high, narrow chest of drawers. The walls were painted a dull khaki green and the curtains were brown.

His dad had plans to extend the house one day, over the garage. It would mean a proper sized room for him. But his dad was almost never there. He worked on the oil rigs, way out at sea. He was gone for weeks and weeks at a time, and when he came back there was so much that Gina wanted doing, or Alice wanted doing, that Dax didn't really get much attention. Besides, his dad always looked so exhausted when he came back that Dax was glad to be the only one who didn't add to it. So his tiny room looked set to stay tiny. Dax told himself it was like a den. Like a fox hole. At night, when his letterbox window was tilted open, Dax could sometimes hear foxes in the woods at the edge of the estate.

And more than once he'd heard the foxes in the garden. You could smell, sometimes, that a fox had been through. In the garden shed, Dax could smell it now. A hot, sour, almost grassy smell. Dax wasn't sure whether he liked it or not, but mixed in with the woody smell of the little hut, it was oddly comforting.

As the late morning wore into afternoon, the sun came out, and the little shed grew very hot. Dax began to get thirsty. He was hungry, but being thirsty was worse. His tongue felt like sandpaper in his mouth. He remembered reading somewhere that nomads crossing the desert used to suck stones to keep their tongues from drying out. He thought seriously about sucking one of the stubby little screws in his father's toolbox, behind the peat bags. He would, soon, if this didn't get better.

He looked up to one of the little wooden shelves and thought about the bottles there. Two were dark green and very dusty. One was clear glass, with a lemonade label on it. It almost certainly *wasn't* lemonade. It was practically certain to be white spirit or turpentine or something else that would burn your tongue off if you tried to drink it, but still, to see it there, looking so *much* like lemonade, as the shed grew hotter and hotter, and the sweat began to make his T-shirt stick to his back, was torture.

For a while, Dax kept his mind off the bottle and its contents of almost certainly *not* lemonade, by doing little drawings of a fox on the chipboard floor of the shed with a bit of old red brick.

The fox stood, with one paw raised, bushy tail out straight, its furry neck craned round and its sharp nose pointing back over its shoulder, as if suddenly called by someone. It wasn't bad. Dax was quite a good artist. His teacher had said he should try for art school one day.

Gina had snorted when she'd heard that. As far as she was concerned, Dax was going to stop sponging and start working for his keep as soon as he turned sixteen. The world had enough charcoal drawings of boats and oil paintings of eagles, thanks very much!

The fox looked and looked, back over its shoulder. Dax stared hard at it, ignoring the little sploshes of sweat that were now dripping off his face.

He felt his eyeballs getting hot, he stared so hard. The fox began to slide across the woodchip. It slithered, quivered, waved in the heat haze, seemed to flick its eye back towards Dax. In the distance, he could *hear* a fox bark, high and shrill. Through the gap in the planks at the back end of the shed, that acid stink of wild dog pulsed through on a draught.

Dazed and drugged by the heat and the smell and the brick outline of the fox that waved and shimmied across the floor, Dax suddenly snapped his head up in a panic.

The air felt hot and thick in his throat. He dug his fingers hard into the chunk of brick, trying to ward off the panic, but it just kept rising. He had to get a drink. He *had* to!

Madly, stupidly, Dax leapt up and lunged at the high wooden shelf. One of the green dusty bottles fell off and hit him hard on the bridge of his nose, sending a bullet of coppery taste to the back of his throat. A large, dead spider, folded into a crunchy spinning wheel, fell onto the red-brick fox with a papery thud. Dax thought, oddly, of brazil nuts. Even as these things happened, his hands had fumbled across to the white glass bottle, with the faded lemonade label, and were twisting the dusty screw cap off the top. It was on tight . . . maybe it was fresh, unopened, wet sweet lemonade! It would be hot, but it would be *wet*. It would be a *drink*.

At the third twist, the loose metal ring beneath the cap scored a fine cut into Dax's right palm, and then the top gave. The bottle made a small popping noise, as if it was, indeed, full of lemonade. But the hot scent it punched up into air was not lemonade. It was white spirit. It hit Dax right between the eyes, making them water and his nose fill up with an unbearable tickling sensation. An unexpectedly forceful sob came out along with his sneeze. He dropped the bottle, and the smell of white spirit rose like an evil gas, cutting across every other scent in the shed. The spirit that hit the bottom of his jeans felt at first shockingly cool, and then began to get warmer and warmer.

Dax felt dizzy and sick. He knew he was going to

faint when a sound like taps being turned on to their very fullest swept into his head. His last thought before he fell was that he ought to get his nose out of the gap in the planks at the back of the shed, to get to fresh air. Or he would possibly never wake up again.

2

Outside the little shed were eight or nine unevenly laid paving slabs. They were big and dull grey, with tiny crumbly pyramids made by ants poking up here and there in the gaps between them. The ants were the only interesting thing about the slabs of concrete. Alice occasionally burned them to death with her magnifying glass.

In the October afternoon, as the sun was slowly beginning to sink in the sky and the midges had begun their teatime dance, daintily bouncing up and down in their little clouds over the compost heap, it began to rain. The cool drops hitting the warm paving slabs made a pleasing pit-a-pat sound, Dax thought dreamily, his snout pushed right out of the gap in the wooden planks at the back of the shed. The ants were completely panicked, as a polka-dot pattern spread across the grey concrete plains between their crumbly earth pyramids.

Soon all the dots were joining up and the paving slabs were a darker grey, with a damp sheen to it. They smelt like hot paving stone tea. They smelt of 'end of playtime'. All the children in the street, one by one, would be called indoors, like the ants which were now frenziedly bolting down the holes between the tiny chunks of earth-boulder that made their shaky pyramid homes.

These thoughts rose up and spread across Dax's mind in a pleasant, warm drift as he woke. He realized that the evil vapour of white spirit inside the shed had gone. Or perhaps it was because he *had* managed to get his face to the gap when he'd fallen. No—he'd done better than that: his whole *head* was outside the shed. Blimey. How had he managed *that*?

Carefully, he pulled his head back in and looked back over his furry red shoulder. The shed was definitely *taller* than he thought it had been. One thing hadn't changed though. He was still desperately thirsty and, now, even more desperately hungry. He could smell something like brazil nuts. Ah. There it was—little wheel thing on the floor. Dax scooped it up on to his tongue and flicked it back into his mouth, munching it down in a couple of seconds. Yep. Very like a rather papery brazil nut.

He paused. Looked down at his feet and then, before he would allow the really BIG thought into his head—the thought which had been hammering at a window in his mind with increasing alarm ever since he'd woken up—Dax thought on *this*.

I . . . he thought to himself, *. . . have just, willingly—and with some enjoyment—eaten a dead spider.*

A flicker of horror ran up the inside of Dax's spine, hitting his throat and making him cough and choke, and then splitting up and shuddering off down each of his limbs and up the back of his neck. The thick hair there was standing on end.

13

Oh—eugh! Eugh! NO! Dax spluttered. A spider! A *spider*? What on earth had made him do *that*?

Worse still was the thought that, if there had been another paper spider wheel on the floor—or even a *living* one, trotting across it—he'd eat that too. It didn't taste at all bad, and he was a very hungry boy.

Now the *BIG* thought demanded, quite crossly, to have the window opened and be let in. 'Aha! But you,' it said, sarcastically, 'are *not* a boy. Are you?'

Dax pulled the hot air in quickly through his snout and did a little sideways dance of shock. It was true enough. His face was long and pointed. His nose was a glistening black, with a delicate spray of black whiskers on either side. The fur around them was white, and Dax could just see, before he went cross-eyed, that it turned to a rich red brown further up his snout. He could feel the way his long tongue settled comfortably between sharp teeth. He used it to test how pointed his fangs were. Whoa! They were pretty impressive.

His feet—well, what *had* been his hands and his feet— were now four paws, with small black claws, scratching slightly on the wooden floor of the shed. The rust-red fur darkened to a deep brown as it went down his legs and almost to black at his feet. He lifted one paw and turned it so he could just see the underside of his new feet. Fleshy pads—black tinged with pink—were fringed with his darkest fur, the black nails curving up from the edges of them into refined points. He flexed them and they moved fluidly, luxuriously.

A rustling noise behind him made him jump again—he rose high off his feet, so much lighter than Dax the boy. Snapping his head round, he saw immediately, and with some pride, the source of the noise. Brushing against some old paper sacking in the corner was the most glorious, thick, bushy fox tail. Its fur graduated from deep red-brown to pale orange and almost to white at the tip. Dax gazed at it in wonder, waving it gently from the strong muscle at the rump for a full minute.

It was a bit of a shock, he told himself, to discover unexpectedly that you were a fox. Pretty shocking to find you could eat dead spiders (or live ones) too. Strangely, though, he didn't feel sick or panicky any more. He felt a heck of a lot better than he had half an hour ago, when he'd been a boy. Every part of his body seemed vital and alive; he could *feel* the taut, lean muscles in his limbs, working smoothly as he turned round in the small wooden hut. He felt well-oiled, slick and healthy.

His hearing was amazing; he could make out a dozen different things at once: the gentle patter of the rain on the shed roof was woven into the flutter of small birds in the shrubs; the drone of several different types of insect dodging the water drops; and the far-off hum and clatter of human life . . . cars, children, washing machines, and TVs, Dax could hear it all.

And his already sharp sense of smell was now quite incredible. He could smell *everything*. The creosote on the wood in the shed mingled with the last traces of the white spirit, the dust, the damp, mildewy creases of the sunshade, folded up like a large green and white bat in the corner, unused for weeks (it had been a wet summer), the rain on the hot paving stones, the ash from last week's bonfire, even now transforming into a gluey black puddle behind the shed, someone's curry, cooking in a nearby kitchen, the sickly, yet somehow *golden* smell of the big communal bins over in the yard that the houses in their street backed on to.

This smell suddenly made him aware again how hungry and thirsty he was. Fine, thought Dax. I'm a fox. I'll think about *why* later. Right now, there are more important things to see to. Quickly, he turned and headed for the gap again. His hearing was picking up the faintest of movements around him in the shed, and his sharp snout was getting that nutty smell again. The boy Dax, inside the fox Dax, made a decision. No more spiders. Get out now before the fox Dax overruled him and licked up a few of those spindly ones that always crouch and shiver in the corners.

His whiskers, grazing the edges of the broken plank hole, told him he *could* squeeze through—just. Partly through instinct and partly through a dim memory of his book of English mammals (long gone to the jumble sale), he knew that his whiskers were a measuring device. If they could clear a gap, so could the rest of him.

Dax paused at the hole. His sharp senses told him there were plenty of humans about, but not in this garden. He lowered his head and pushed through. The rest of his sleek body lowered, stretched, and followed without a struggle. He was out.

A cool gust of wind and a spatter of rain ruffled the fur around his eyes. He looked quickly from left to right and then shot down the garden to where it ended in a low brambly hedge. Fortunately, the hedge backed partly on to the yard containing the communal bins, and partly on to the perimeter of some wasteland which sloped down to the local allotments. The allotments gave on to a small copse. He slid under the hedge and viewed his options. To his right was the wasteland—a bare two or three hundred metres to run across until he reached the cover of the allotments and the copse beyond. To his left were the large, overflowing, communal bins.

The stench of these bins, at this end of the week, just before the bin men came on Monday, was thick and heavy. Gina often complained to the council about it. Dax was aware of the stench, but this time it was different. It was revolting, yes, but at the same time—*golden*. Filled with promise. Dax the fox *knew* that it was full of food. Old biscuits, bread, cold, squashed tea bags curled into half full packets of damp crisps, bacon rind, apple cores, the ketchup-soaked ends of fish fingers spat out by toddlers, the lard-lined corners of empty corned-beef cans, sticky spare ribs and chicken—oh—above all *chicken*. Somewhere, quite near the surface, he could smell fried chicken, the kind that's dipped in breadcrumbs and a top secret blend of herbs and spices. *Chicken . . .* In those bins wasn't rubbish at all. It was *treasure*.

But there was a more urgent need. First he *had* to get a drink. His fox tongue was curling inside his mouth, dry and rasping. A muddy ditch hemmed the edge of the wasteland and he could smell water pooled there, distinct from the smell of the rain. Decided, he crawled out to his right and trotted swiftly along, keeping low and close to the hedge. Within seconds he'd found an old tyre, up-ended in the ditch with a glinting black well of water resting in its curve. The water tasted better than it smelt. Dax lapped up nearly all of it, ignoring one or two insects struggling on its surface. The aftertaste of burnt rubber wasn't great, but it was such a relief to get some water into his parched body that Dax didn't care.

The light was fading fast now, which made him feel easier. There didn't seem to be anybody about anyway, but Dax the fox's instinct told him the darker it was, the safer it was. He glanced around the familiar patch of wasteland, which seemed now so different, and seeing nobody, skirted the hedge back towards the bins.

A small mountain of refuse, in black bin bags, in boxes, or in supermarket carrier bags, rose up in an unsteady slope to the mouth of the bins. The three huge grey metal cylinders were topped with heavy black plastic flip lids, which were almost never shut. Far too much rubbish was stuffed into the bins for the lids ever to close, so people just dumped their bin bags, boxes, and carriers on the sticky concrete around them, until the mountain rose high enough to meet the lip of each container.

It was perfect. Dax nimbly scaled the mountain to the top of the nearest bin and began to scrabble at the peak. His sharp claws cut easily through a bulging plastic sack, causing a small eruption of potato peelings, baked beans, and two pink-spattered yoghurt pots. Underneath them, though—treasure! The red and white stripes of the box confirmed what his clever nose had told him— fried chicken! Dax seized the box in his jaws and carried it back down the rubbish mountain, sliding gently in a slick of melted ice cream. In a second he was back under the bush and tearing through the cardboard.

In the unlikely event that Dax ever got to eat fried chicken takeaway, he knew that you had to pick at it carefully with your fingers and teeth, avoiding the knuckles of the bones and the dark, greasy undercarriage of the ribs. He recoiled from the skin and the pink, stretchy veins. There would usually be a lemon-scented wet-wipe to clean yourself up afterwards.

Dax the fox didn't care about such delicate ways. The bones, still laden with plenty of meat, were in his mouth instantly. His teeth and tongue worked in an impressive partnership with his paws, shearing off the meat and breadcrumbs, working down the drumsticks until they were clean, and then depositing them back on the thin cardboard. There were four pieces. They were finished within three minutes.

Panting slightly, after the frenzy of eating, Dax checked to see if anyone had noticed him. Still no one about. The water and the chicken were working through his system already and he felt fantastic. But still a little hungry.

The rain had stopped now, but in the last of the day's

light, Dax could see in the ditch below him a number of subterranean dwellers, lured to the surface by the rhythm of the shower. Dax the boy started to protest, but Dax the fox paid him no heed. Stretching forward on to his forepaws, his legs and rump still under cover of the hedge, he used the row of small incisors between his fangs to gently tug on the biggest of the worms. It pulled, stretched like a thick pink rubber band, and then, as he waggled it gently from side to side, more pink, smooth flesh extended out of the loose, wet earth. As its tail finally broke through the soil, it pinged wetly against his nose, curling frenziedly, before Dax gulped it down. It tasted a bit like raw mushroom, with a bitter edge. He went on, methodically harvesting the worms from the soil. After the fourth or fifth, there seemed to be no more. He felt better still. Better? He felt amazing!

After another quick glance to be sure nobody was looking, Dax tensed his muscular haunches, and then launched himself forward and began to run across the wasteland, making for the allotments and the copse beyond.

3

As the tall grass flicked away madly in front of him, Dax sprinted like a bullet across the wasteland. Each paw seemed to push the earth away and send him on a split-second flight with every stride. The evening air whipped into his ears, rippling the soft white fur inside them, and pressed his black whiskers to his cheeks.

He deftly leapt over all obstacles: tussocks of weed growing around the chunks of rough concrete that littered the ground; rolls of rusty chicken-wire fencing; empty paraffin cans; and the wheel-robbed skeletons of abandoned bikes. At the edge of the allotments he slowed and pricked his ears forward. There was every possibility that some gardener would still be toiling on his vegetable patch. Not at this end, though. Further away there was at least one. The smell of human seemed as sharp and distinctive to Dax the fox as the smell of fox had once been to Dax the boy.

Keeping low, he edged swiftly along a row of small sheds, past a netting cage protecting some late raspberries, ducked beneath a water butt raised on bricks, and shot across into the deep wiry grass that rose up at the allotment boundary, in the shadow of the copse. Only when he felt the spongy porridge of the woodland floor did Dax slow down. He was panting and exhilarated. It was like the kind of dream that leaves you smiling and with tears in your eyes when you wake. Except that he *was* awake. He had never felt more awake.

Feeling much safer in the damp warmth of the little wood, Dax sat down, resting his rump comfortably on the peaty earth and curling his fabulous bushy tail around to tickle at his forepaws. He knew he should try to work out what this was all about. He knew he should be feverishly wondering what was going to happen next. And yet now that he'd had food and water and a fantastic flying run across the wasteland, awake as he'd been just ten seconds ago, suddenly all he really wanted was to go to sleep.

Nearby was a fallen oak tree, a victim of the hurricane force winds which had pounded the country around the time he was born; so his dad had told him. As Dax nestled into the hollow in the earth, dug out under one end of the log, he was already drifting away. In the upper layers of sleep, he heard his dad telling him, 'It was a dramatic time, Dax. The wind—blimey—you should've heard the wind. It was wailing and tearing at the building, making the windows rattle and shake. Your mum didn't notice. She had enough problems of her own bringing you into the world, but I'll never forget that wind.'

It was one of their favourite stories, shared very occasionally in the rare times they had alone together. His father always told it as if it was the first time, his pale grey eyes fixed in the distance, remembering.

'And right after you were born, around three or four in the morning, it dropped—just like that! To nothing. It was so silent I could hear you breathing in your little plastic cot. I looked out of the window and there were trees down across the valley. The next day was really strange too. The sun came up red, like a blood orange, and the heat of that day was incredible. It was April, but it was hot enough for June. Weather phenomenon, they called it.'

Dax, his ears still pricked and on duty for any sound but the gentle movement of the woodland, felt himself slide down through another layer of sleep. He felt warm and contented and more at home under the log than he ever had in his little damp box of a bedroom. He was dimly aware of the soft, powdery smell of lilac. He knew it wasn't real; it was October, not April. But the smell came to him when he thought of his mother. It was her scent and one of the handful of things he remembered about her. He'd been only four when she died.

He remembered her smell; the way she would sing to him sometimes. He remembered gurgling with laughter, trying to bite the taut palm of her hand between his toddler teeth, and then getting tickled. Wrapped in warm memory, his tail curled about him, Dax fell deeply asleep.

His first thought was that the high chest of drawers must have tipped over somehow, and landed on him. Something hard and unyielding was pressed on to the back of his head. Dax tried to move, but the weight on his skull was absolutely solid. He took a frightened breath and only when he'd inhaled a few bits of leaf and earth did he remember where he was. He opened his eyes and realized it was dark and damp and he was still in the woodland, jammed under the fallen oak, his nose pressed firmly into the earth. But why was he so squashed, when he'd been perfectly comfortable before, as he'd fallen asleep?

Reaching out, he pulled himself sideways, turning his head to the right, and thankfully, slid out from under the log, grazing the back of his head and his ear. He rose to his knees, groggily, and dusted the leaf and earth matter off his T-shirt and jeans. His hand froze in mid-sweep. It was, oddly, far more of a shock to realize he was a boy again, than it had been to accept he was a fox. Dax sank to a cross-legged position, trying to work it all out. The wood was dark and quiet, but there was a dim orange glow creeping into it from the streetlights far away in his road. He checked his watch; it was only 5.30. It seemed so much later.

Dax thought about the Incredible Hulk. His dad had a stack of old, yellowed comics under the stairs, which featured the Incredible Hulk. In the Incredible Hulk, when scientist David Banner got mad he turned into a huge green giant. His shirt always got all ripped, his shoes vanished—just burst off his feet, Dax supposed—but somehow his trousers and underpants always stayed on, although they ripped into little shreds at the bottom. Probably kids' parents wouldn't have bought them the comic if Hulk's trousers and pants had burst off too, reflected Dax.

So when the Incredible Hulk went away again and David Banner shrank back into an ordinary sized man, he always had his trousers on still. And then he just had to nick a shirt off a clothes line or something, and run home.

Why then, thought Dax, *am I dressed exactly as I was before? Surely I should have just shrugged out of my human clothes when I turned into a fox? Surely my watch should be lying on the shed floor along with my T-shirt, jeans, underpants, socks, and trainers?*

Or maybe it had just been a dream. But if it *had* been only a dream, how could he have got out of the shed? He peered at his watch again. Its luminous hands now pointed to 5.31. Teatime.

Teatime! Oh no! Teatime! Dax leapt to his feet, swaying dazedly, as he remembered that Gina and Alice would be back any time—if they weren't already! The shops shut at 5.30, so even if they weren't back yet they would be, any time now. And if he wasn't back in the garden—back in the *shed*! Not *one* weed had been pulled. Not *one*! Gina would go off like a nuclear bomb if he didn't convince her that he *couldn't* do that weeding, because he was trapped in the shed. He had to get back in there—now!

Dax ran across the wood, jumping over roots and dodging round the trees. He felt heavy and lumpy as a boy, but he tried to *think* like a fox and move as much like one as he could. He pounded out of the trees and across the edge of the allotments, blundering into a corner of the netting round the raspberries and scratching his shoulder badly on one of its little bamboo supports. He crashed on through the wasteland, stumbling through the tangle of weeds, and having to do a little dance in the rusty chicken-wire fencing as it bounced up and snatched at his ankles. He was drenched in a terrified sweat by the time he reached the low brambly hedge. It was a great deal harder getting through it now, as a boy, but he didn't dare to stop and worry about prickles.

By sheer force of will he pushed himself under the vicious barbs, past the remains of his chicken takeaway meal, and back into the garden. He ran so hard to the shed that he actually smacked into it, face on. The lights in the house were still dark—but even as he was letting out a shaky sigh of relief, he saw the double arc of car headlights swinging into the drive at the side of the house. They were back!

With a horrified gasp, Dax dropped to the gap at the back of the shed and was about to push through when he realized he couldn't possibly get back in—he was much too big!

As panic flooded through his head like a blood-red tidal wave, Dax struggled to keep some sense. What now? What now? He glanced wildly around the garden. Over by the compost heap lay a garden fork, its prongs curled up dangerously. He darted across and grabbed it, dragging it back to the shed within seconds. He heard one, then two, car doors slam, and the faint unwelcome jingle of Gina's keys.

Grasping the handle of the fork, Dax shoved it into the gap and pushed it round and across hard, levering the broken plank off its remaining nails. It seemed as if it would never move, although it *couldn't* be as strong as all that! Dax heard the front door crash shut and saw a light shine dimly through from the hallway at the front of the house. He could hear their voices.

Fear was stabbing at him and his heart was racing; Dax put the mad, screaming energy coursing through his body to good use and sent it all down the shaft of the fork in one huge spasm. With a loud crack, the plank split away from its nails and swung sideways. Dax flung the fork back across the garden and ducked down through the larger gap. It was still very tight, and his injured shoulder hurt badly, but he wriggled and pulled and dragged himself back into the shed.

Once he was in, he scrambled around and seized the wonky plank, shoving it back into place. It swung away again, so he hauled the heavy bag of peat across it, pinning it back, hoping that Gina's sharp eyes wouldn't notice anything amiss.

Then he turned, fixed his eyes on the shed door, commanded his breathing to go back to normal, and waited.

Nothing happened.

Gradually his heaving chest subsided and the shaking in his hands settled down to the occasional tremor. As his eyes grew used to the dark, he could make out the things in the shed; things that spoke of a time, just a few hours ago, when something extraordinary had happened. The raffia, the pots, the blurred red-brick drawing of the fox, just about visible in a shaft of light through the small shed window. He shifted and his foot hit the lemonade bottle. It rolled slightly, spilling a few remaining drops of white spirit across the floor. Dax bent and picked it up, returning it to the shelf.

As he brought his arm back down, the shed door opened.

4

Gina looked Dax up and down before she spoke, and for one mad second he thought she might be about to ask if he was OK.

'What happened?' she demanded, her eyes raking over him and the shed around him. He was drenched with sweat and shaking, but now he tried to look groggy too.

'The wind blew the door shut,' he mumbled, 'and then the latch fell down. I've been stuck in here since just after you left.'

She regarded him for a moment and he couldn't tell what she was thinking. After perhaps ten seconds she simply drew a short breath and turned back up the garden path.

'Don't just stand there, then,' she said, over her shoulder. 'Come in and get your tea.'

In the kitchen, Alice was at the table wearing a new pink fur thing. He guessed it was a sort of waistcoat but Alice said, proudly, that it was a bolero, which sounded to Dax like something used to hold back traffic. Frankly, it was better suited to holding back traffic. But Alice was in a good mood and quite friendly as Dax got himself a glass of water, twisting on the tap with a shaky hand.

'We saw Kelly at The Sphinx,' she chattered (The Sphinx was the daftest name imaginable for an English shopping centre), 'and I'm going to a sleepover party with her next week. Sorry, Dax, you can't come. Boys aren't allowed.'

Dax snorted suddenly into his water, and choked slightly. Not at the thought of going to a sleepover party with Alice and all her little pink friends, but because he'd just noticed what tea was. Red and white striped boxes sat on the tea table—it was takeaway fried chicken. Dax began to giggle, which made Alice and Gina stare. Dax wasn't generally given to giggling in their company.

'What's wrong with you, boy?' snapped Gina and peered at him hard. In the bright glare of the kitchen light, his scratched and grubby face was obvious. 'What's *this*?' she demanded and strode across to poke him hard on his wounded shoulder, where a little flower of blood had bloomed through his sleeve. 'What were you doing in that shed?'

'I—I—nothing,' stammered Dax. 'I just fell over in it. I . . . sort of fainted. It was very hot.'

Gina looked at him hard and her face was impossible to read. Maybe she was about to strike him, or maybe smile and say 'never mind'. Perhaps she was worried about what his father might think. Dad was due home in a few days and the bruises might still show.

'Eat your food,' she said shortly. 'And then get yourself cleaned up. You stink like a dog.'

Dax, still working hard to stop grinning, sat down

and polished off his second fried chicken takeaway that day. Taken away from a shop rather than a bin this time, but still tasting much the same. After tea he got into the shower and after the shower he got straight into bed. He was extremely tired and achy, as if he'd run a marathon. His very bones felt sore. And they should. They'd shrunk and twisted and turned themselves into fox bones not three hours ago—and then back to boy bones again. People told you about growing up and how it did odd things to you, reflected Dax, like growing hair under your arms and your voice changing. But no one had thought to tell him, 'Oh . . . and by the way—sometimes you turn into a fox.'

It wasn't something they put helpful posters about up on the walls at school. A tired, mad little giggle eased out of Dax as he got sleepier. He pictured the poster. BOYS, it read, HAVING FOX PROBLEMS? CAN'T STOP SCAVENGING ON TIPS AND EATING SPIDERS? COME AND SEE THE SCHOOL COUNSELLOR . . .

Dax thought he heard the shrill scream of a distant vixen in the woods as he drifted off to sleep, still laughing.

And, of course, the next morning he was even more inclined to think it was all a dream. It must have been. The hurt shoulder *had* happened when he'd fainted and he'd just had an amazing dream.

But before he left for school, on a cool, grey morning, he found an excuse to walk down the garden, and with a pulse of excitement, he saw clearly the broken plank at the back of the shed, and the scattered chicken bones and squashed box under the hedge. How had he managed *that,* if it was just a dream?

Clive met him at the gate as he arrived at school. Clive's glasses were bent again and his Monday morning jumper, which should have been clean and ironed, was scrunched up and had muddy stains on it. Dax looked at his friend closely and saw his eyes were still wet. He gave him a bit of tissue from his pocket as they headed into the school. There was nothing he needed to say. Clive had just had another smacking from Toby Rogers and Matthew Spacey. Clive told him they'd found out where he lived and were waiting for him at the bottom of his road.

'I don't mind getting thumped at school,' he said, daftly, because of course he *did* mind. 'But I just can't stand it when they're outside my house too.'

'Are you going to tell?' asked Dax, although he knew what the answer would be. Clive eyed him as if he'd gone mad. He was a small boy, smaller than Dax, and clever. He was extremely good at science and maths and he talked way too posh for a boy at Bark's End Junior School. Clive had a quite unintentional habit of *looking* posh, too, which didn't help. He carried an old-fashioned brown satchel, rather than a backpack, and wore knitted v-neck jumpers and a tie, when he could have worn a school sweatshirt and polo top instead. He was asking for it, really, as far as Toby and Matthew were concerned. So far this term, they'd smacked him with large beans off the Indian bean tree in the upper school playground, wrecked his scale model of a steamship and its mechanical workings which he'd spent hours on for a class project, held his head down the toilet bowl and flushed it, upended him in a bin, and shoved itchy rosehip seeds down his shirt countless times.

Dax tried to help. He was the one who ended up sloshing water down Clive's back to get the seeds off and handing him the paper towels to dry his recently flushed hair. He'd spoken up boldly for Clive once or twice, answering back when Toby and Matthew were jeering at him, and got clouted on the nose for his efforts. Clive told him not to bother.

'Look,' he said, sagely, 'this is what school *is* for me. I just have to get through it. One day I'll be at college and then at university and then I'll have a really high up job and I'll hire Toby and Matthew to concrete the drive outside my mansion house, and when they're not looking I'll spit in their tea and rub their chocolate biscuits over the cat.'

Dax laughed until he cried. Clive could be so funny, without even trying. And it was true, he'd been enduring regular bruisings from Toby and Matthew and other part-time bullies for all his school life. Some things you just got used to.

But one day people may go too far. And for Clive it was that Thursday.

'That's fantastic! Really, the best I've ever seen!' Mrs Radway beamed at Clive, who was pink in the face and delighted that his work was top of the class again. He'd just handed in another working model—a perfect clock, engineered from paper. It was an astounding thing, thought Dax, as Mrs Radway held it up and turned it gently under the fluorescent light above the classroom. Cut into precise cogs and levers from fine green card and pasted carefully together—it actually *worked*.

'Clive, I'd like you to take this right down to Mr Clegg now,' said Mrs Radway. 'I think he should see what a clever boy you are.'

Don't teachers ever *think*? wondered Dax, as he heard Toby and Matthew sniggering. Don't they ever think about what's going to happen *after* they've said stuff like that? Clive was too thrilled to notice, but Dax could not only hear and feel the danger building up in the desks behind him, he could actually *smell* it. Hostility, resentment, and violence leaked out of Toby's and Matthew's skin like an evil fog and wafted down the aisles between the desks, snaking towards Clive.

Poor Clive literally *skipped* as he headed to the door with his paper clock. And maybe that was the final straw. Toby and Matthew got up with the rest of the class as the bell rang for break, and then charged through the door after him.

In the confusion of each class emptying itself into the long school corridor, Toby and Matthew could no longer be seen; nor could Clive. It didn't matter to Dax. He could smell them. Their scent led away towards the head teacher's office and he hoped that maybe they wouldn't have the nerve to chase Clive too far in *that* direction. Suddenly, Dax picked up another, sharp, hot scent—it was one of panic and it came from Clive. He pushed hard through the swarm of children and tried to run but then drew to a halt and turned his head to the right. There was no classroom or exit to the playground, but a dull, blue-painted door, normally locked solidly against pupils. He knew it led down a short flight of concrete steps to the school basement, which housed the boiler and the caretaker's tools and cleaning equipment. Dax shoved the door hard and found he was right; the door swung open and a dim light shone up from the underground gloom.

Dax ran down the stairs and nearly slid, halfway, over some pieces of green card. With a groan, he knelt and picked up one or two shreds of Clive's wonderful paper clock. Anger punched into him and he yelled: 'Clive! Where are you?!' His sharp hearing immediately picked up a small whimper, followed by a snigger and a scuffle. Dax thundered on down into the basement and saw Clive wedged into a foot-high gap under the boiler, curled up on his side. Someone had yanked out his tie and shoved a rancid looking mop-head down the front of his shirt. There was a little smudge of dark red under his nose and the ancient dust under his cheek was congealing into a damp sludge where tears had trickled into it.

Dax was appalled. Fresh fury shot through him and he glanced around for Clive's attackers. Clive was saying now, raspily: 'Don't, Dax. Dax, just go. I'm OK.'

The absurdity of his words stung Dax into action and he grabbed a short piece of wood from the floor and charged around the basement, clattering into old boxes and steel buckets and snake-like coils of hosepipe.

'Where are you?!' he shrieked. 'Come out, you stinking cowards!'

'And you'll do *what*?' Toby stepped out of the gloom, smirking across his thick, ugly face. Matthew sidled out next to him, his good-looking features blighted by his natural nastiness.

Dax heard his voice strangling in his throat as he said, 'I'll show you what.'

Clive cried out, 'Dax—*don't*! Just go!'

As he raised the wood Dax saw a flicker of confusion, rather than fear, in Toby's eyes. 'Oh, yeah—right—*I'm* scared,' chortled Matthew.

Dax brought the wood down as hard as he could in the direction of Toby's head. It cracked against him, but it was the boy's hand that had caught the blow—a large, thick hand, like its large, thick owner, which was even now clenching on to Dax's piece of wood and twisting it out of his grasp. Dax didn't have time to step back before the wood struck him across the cheek. Toby played cricket and all his expertise went into the swing. Dax was pole-axed. As he tipped back and fell onto a narrow strip of stone floor behind the boiler, he could already smell his own blood, and the wave of rage that plunged down over him just before the back of his head hit, was like nothing he'd ever known.

It couldn't have been more than ten seconds, but to Dax it seemed longer and slower. He could feel the muggy heat at the base of the old boiler and smell the sharp iron scent of blood in his nose; he could feel his skin stretching and swelling around the impact point on his cheek; he could hear Clive whimpering again and Toby saying, 'That'll sort him out. *He* started it. Mate— you live by the sword, you die by the sword.'

'Live by the plank, die by the plank,' added Matthew and the pair began sniggering helplessly.

Dax's skin was tingling weirdly all over. For a while his vision swam into inky blackness and the sound of taps turned on to their fullest was back in his ears and then he was lying on his belly, looking under the base of the boiler to the back of Clive's head and watching Toby's and Matthew's school shoes walk by, and pause by their victim. Maybe that would've been that, if Dax hadn't then seen one of each pair of scuffed black lace-ups senselessly give Clive a vicious kick.

Dax screamed. The sound was so high and wild and loud that it scared even him. But the scream was only the start. His sleek auburn body curled around the boiler and then sprang at the two boys. There was a blur of grey and red and then Dax realized he wasn't the only one screaming. His claws found cloth and skin and hair, his teeth found flailing limbs and contorted faces; the wildness that stormed through him poured out on to Toby and Matthew as they cried out and stumbled and sobbed, clawing desperately at the thing that was

37

attacking them, trying to get back up the basement steps.

'Help me! Help me!' cried Matthew. 'It's a monster! Mum! Mum!' Toby just kept up a high-pitched wail and tried feebly to beat Dax off his shoulder as he staggered up the steps.

The pandemonium grew louder and more desperate and Dax felt his teeth pierce skin. Suddenly, the boy inside him registered revulsion at the thought of tasting this hateful creature's blood. He dropped to the floor and slid back into the shadows, panting, watching as the two boys literally crawled up the steps, crying. Bloodied, scratched, and with large ragged tears in their sweatshirts and trousers, they finally reached the door at the top and, clinging to each other, pushed it open and fell out of the basement. The door swung shut again behind them and silence descended.

5

As his panting subsided, Dax became aware of someone else shakily breathing above the low hum of the boiler. Clive! With a pang of regret, Dax realized that the whole scene must have been terrifying for his friend. He needed to check on Clive—but he also needed to get away before he was caught. Raising his fine black snout, he sensed a stream of fresh, outside air and followed it, his claws making a dainty sound on the concrete floor. The stream led him to a long, shallow, open window above a stack of old wooden chairs. It lay at ground level on the outside, but was about five feet up from the basement floor. As far as Dax could remember, it gave on to a small patch of ground by the school bins, well away from the playground. Behind this area was a high beech hedge, bordering a road. And on the far end of the road was a churchyard and some trees—good fox cover. All he'd have to do is get down the road.

'Dax? Dax—are you there?' Clive's voice sounded thin and wavery, but better than Dax might have hoped for. Glancing up once more at his exit, Dax trotted back round to Clive, still wedged at the base of the boiler, and looked down at him. Clive's eyes stretched open in fear and Dax realized the boy thought he might attack him too. He smiled reassuringly, but then guessed this might actually look quite scary on a fox's snout, so he stopped smiling and instead dropped his nose to Clive's damp forehead and gave it a little nudge. He wondered whether to try to speak, but felt sure that he couldn't. And anyway, a talking fox would surely freak anyone.

Clive was gazing at him in amazement. Dax stepped back and once again studied his escape route. He could scale the chairs easily and be out in three seconds. Clive saw the fox look back at him, turn its head quizzically to one side and, in a very unfoxlike fashion, nod at him. Then it was gone.

Outside, Dax crouched behind the bins for a while, sniffing the air and trying to work out how close any humans were. The air was teeming with people smells and he knew that breaking cover even for a few seconds was a huge risk, but now that he was thinking more calmly, he realized that lunch break would be over soon and if he hadn't returned to class there'd be trouble. He also badly wanted to see Clive back at his desk, cleaned up and calmed down. About Toby and Matthew he didn't care in the least.

Although this was only the second time it had happened to him, again he felt oddly at ease with the mad idea of being a fox. It felt far more natural than being a boy. As a boy he felt weak, out of balance, but as a fox everything flowed. He also couldn't help feeling a bit impressed with his strength. He wasn't a large fox, but he'd bested two of the biggest school bullies, no problem! Although, he reflected, he'd had the advantage of surprise and scaring the wits out of them. Two large boys *were* capable of doing him damage if they were ready, so he shouldn't get cocky.

But no, he needed to get back. He needed to turn back into Dax the boy. But how? Still hidden behind the bins, Dax closed his eyes and furrowed his foxy brow, focusing as hard as he could on turning back into a boy again. After several seconds, nothing happened. This decided Dax. He couldn't stay here. By now Matthew and Toby could have told everyone there was a wild animal in the basement (although how they'd explain what they and Clive were doing down there, he didn't know) and the caretaker could be searching the area at this moment. Dax took one more look, saw no one, and belted across to the beech hedge. He skirted it as far as he could, masking himself from the road, before the perimeter ended and he had to crawl under it.

There was a stretch of quiet residential street on the other side. Down to the right the road ended in a rough grassy path that led into the churchyard. With another glance to be sure nobody was about, Dax ran towards it. The only witness, as far as he could tell, was a small girl of about three, who sat on a wheeled toy cow on the other side of her garden gate with a handful of bread and jam and her little mouth and eyes wide open.

''Ox! 'Ox! Mummy! 'Ox!' she shouted, stickily.

'Yes, sweetheart,' said her mum from inside the house, clearly not looking.

Dax reached the churchyard in seconds. Inside was a haven of tall grass around unkempt gravestones, thick hawthorn hedges, and dense green yew trees which had been allowed to spread. Inside one of the yews, Dax found a safe green cave. A startled wren chirped and then fled for its life. Dax *was* a bit hungry, but more than that, he now needed sleep. It was the kind of need for sleep that you get after a big shock or a terrible row or even a terrific surprise. This is quite normal for humans—but far more so for foxes. With the danger now past, Dax really did need to sleep. He was also aware that he might change back into a boy if he did, so he checked that he could get back out of the yew, boy sized, and thought he probably could.

The grey clouds had lifted and early afternoon sun filtered into his dark green cave in thin pale shafts, warming the back of his furry head as Dax curled his tail around his paws. Small birds cheeped anxiously in the bushes nearby, scenting the predator. A lorry rumbled on a distant road. Dax fell asleep.

At half-past one, Mrs Radway was just saying, 'And where on earth is Dax Jones, Clive?' when Dax walked in. Clive was back at his desk, looking pale, but surprisingly neat after his lunch hour of terror.

'Sorry, miss,' said Dax. 'I was feeling a bit sick and I couldn't leave the toilets.'

'Another one!' said Mrs Radway, shaking her head and turning to pick up the whiteboard marker. 'Is there a plague at this school today? Sickness, screaming, wild animal sightings!'

Dax stiffened and glanced urgently at Clive as he sat down at his desk. Clive stared back at him but his face gave nothing away. Dax realized that Toby and Matthew were not in the room.

He'd managed to clean up in the cloakroom before dashing back to class, and was relieved to see there was just a small bruise on his cheek, considering the whack it had received from a plank of wood, not forty-five minutes ago. His foxnap had lasted only twenty minutes and he'd woken up a boy, with time to get back into class without too much attention being paid to him. He was desperate to know what had happened to Clive and Matthew and Toby, but had to remain seated, pretending to pay attention to Mrs Radway all afternoon, before he could find out anything.

At last the final school bell went and everyone trooped out. Clive didn't look at Dax; he just went to his peg and collected his coat and bag. Dax waited behind him as he did up the toggles on his navy duffle. Clive was going so slowly that Dax thought he was playing some kind of waiting game with him, but after a while he realized that his friend was probably in shock and *couldn't* go any faster. When Clive finally turned towards him his face was paler then ever and his dark grey eyes luminous and wary.

'What happened to you—after I left?' asked Dax.

Clive didn't answer. He just started walking towards

the school exit. Dax was perplexed. This was very unlike Clive. He followed the boy and grabbed his shoulder. 'Clive! What happened? Where's Matthew and Toby?'

Clive stopped and turned to look hard at Dax. 'You don't know then? You weren't there?' Now he was biting down hard on his lower lip.

Dax wasn't sure how to go on. Had Clive worked out that *he* was the fox? Probably not. He probably thought Dax had just legged it when things got scary. 'Just tell me what happened, Clive,' he coaxed.

Clive turned and began walking again. 'Toby and Matthew have gone home. Their mums were called in to pick them up. They say a rabid wolf or something attacked them in the cellar while they were looking for the caretaker.'

Clive trudged on out of the school doorway and across the rapidly emptying playground. 'Nobody else witnessed the incident,' he went on, impassively, as if he were reading a news report, 'but the boys were covered in scratches and blood and in a state of shock. The wild animal hasn't been found.'

'And what about you?' asked Dax. 'What happened to your paper clock?'

'I managed to fall over in the playground and mash up my clock. I was so upset I spent the lunch hour in the toilets. Just like you.' Clive turned and looked searchingly at Dax. 'Just like you,' he said again.

Dax badly wanted to be truthful to Clive. He'd been longing, for the past three days, to share his fox secret

with someone, but had decided he would never be
believed. Now, though . . .

'Clive . . . ' he hesitated, unsure how to go on. 'Did—
did *you* see the wild animal?'

'Yes, I did,' said Clive. 'But it was just a fox. Didn't
you see it?'

Dax simply didn't know what to say, and in the event
he said nothing, because Clive suddenly sped away out
of the school gates without looking back. Dax made no
attempt to chase after him. As he left the playground he
was aware of two or three groups of children hanging
back, still talking about Toby and Matthew. His sharp
hearing picked up their awed conversations.

' . . . covered in scratches and bleeding and *crying* like
babies!'

' . . . they were screaming! I heard them! They said
there was a monster in the basement. They had to go
home with their mums!'

' . . . a wolf or a fox or a dog or something. But a giant
one, like out of *The Hound of the Baskervilles*.'

'I reckon someone finally got even with them. Maybe
it was the caretaker. They tipped over his bins last week.
Good on him, I reckon.'

Dax couldn't help smiling to himself as he walked
up the hill away from Bark's End Junior School. He
didn't know what the results of today's work would be,
but it would surely be worth it! Part of him, he had to
admit, couldn't wait to see Toby and Matthew come back
tomorrow. How would they live this down?

'What happened to your face?' asked Alice, glancing up from her mermaid doll, which she had been forcing to swim in the kitchen sink. It was an eerie scene. The doll's plastic smile and wide, bright blue eyes managed to look extremely panicky, staring up through the washing-up, and its tail was caught on a fork.

'Walked into something,' said Dax. 'Where's G— where's Mum?'

'Talking to someone in the front room,' said Alice, holding up the dripping mermaid doll. 'He's come about you.'

'What? Who?' demanded Dax, thinking wildly that it might be Toby's or Matthew's dad, come to complain. But then, that was ridiculous. What would they say? 'I'm sorry, Mrs Jones, but you just can't let your boy go morphing into a fox and biting my son whenever he likes! He needs a firmer hand!' In spite of his nerves, Dax laughed to himself. No, there wasn't much danger of *that*.

He walked down the hallway silently and peered through the crack of the front room door. He could just make out a tall man, with dark, curly hair that hung to his shoulders. It looked odd because he was wearing a suit, and the hair didn't really seem to match it. The man, as far as he could tell, was writing on a sheaf of papers and offering one across to Gina. From the tone of Gina's voice, he could tell she was in awe of this person. He must be someone important. Dax listened hard to catch the drift of their words.

'Well, Mr Hind, I must say I'm surprised. I mean, we

know he's a bright boy, and I've always made sure he did his homework and tried hard at school, I pride myself on that, but—really—he's a genius?'

Dax gasped. What on earth was this? But the man cut in.

'Well, it's not exactly that, Mrs Jones. In those tests I was telling you about, we discovered a small number of children who are showing unique signs of ability. It may not even have been obvious in normal schooling, but our people know these signs and think it's vital to sort these special children out from the rest and give them the kind of education which will nurture those unique abilities.'

'Well!' Gina exhaled and paused. Then, 'But will it cost us anything?' (Typical! thought Dax.) 'I mean, of course we want the best for Dax, but we haven't got much money and it's hard enough just keeping up with his ordinary school clothes and books and PE kit and stuff.'

'No, Mrs Jones. It won't cost you a penny. The government believes that every one of these special children will more than pay back its investment. All we need from you is your consent.'

'Well—I'll have to speak to his father. Although I'm sure he'll agree. He's away on the rigs most of the time, so it's not like he's going to miss the boy.' Dax felt a small stab of hurt at this, but guessed it was true. 'Dax!' she suddenly yelled and he jumped violently.

After a brief pause in which he edged backwards up the hall, Dax called back, 'Hi! I'm home.'

'Come in,' called Gina in her sweet (and completely fake) voice. 'There's someone here to see you, darling.' Darling? She *must* have been impressed.

Dax stepped into the front room and the stranger put down his papers and stood up, holding out his right hand for Dax to shake. He was tall and well built and his eyes were the most piercing blue Dax had ever seen. His hand was warm and leathery; an outdoors kind of hand. Dax looked searchingly at his face, which was good-looking and tanned.

'I'm Owen Hind,' the man said and there was a faint West Country edge to his accent. 'I work for the education department. Dax—we've noticed that you're a bit different.'

6

Dax looked at Owen Hind sharply. He couldn't *possibly* know, and yet—and there was his searching look while he went on and on about government tests and how Dax had shown up as something exceptional, and was to be 'hot-housed' with some other equally 'special' children. Owen Hind was studying him intently throughout his speech and Dax felt fear and excitement fizzing through him in equal measure. Something was happening here. Something *other*.

They sat down and talked some more. Dax, it turned out, was to go away this very weekend to join the other students at Tregarren College in Cornwall, if his mum agreed. (She would, thought Dax, wryly.) The man showed Dax a series of official looking bits of paper with a government seal at the top of each page. Gina absorbed herself in reading through all the small print, and it obviously met with her approval, because she kept nodding and smiling excitedly.

Dax asked, several times, exactly *how* it was that the department of education thought he was exceptional, and every time Owen Hind fudged him with the kind of meaningless babble that you hear on TV talk shows; talk of 'indefinable but exciting potential' and 'special qualities' and 'exceptional and outstanding hallmarks' of something or the other. Dax was more and more certain that the man was bluffing, but he smiled and said he'd be delighted to go to the college, if his mum and dad thought it was best for him. What else could he do? Could it be any worse than living with Gina and Alice, wondering where the next slap or locking out was coming from? More than that, his recent adventures had given him a taste for the unknown. If the worst came to the worst, he could always do the fox thing and run off (he hoped—he still wasn't certain about this).

Owen left them with more papers to look over, and contact numbers at the department of education to check his credentials. As he shook Gina's hand, he said he would be happy to drive Dax to Cornwall himself, this very weekend. It all seemed highly suspicious to Dax. Whoever heard of an offer of a place in an exclusive school starting—*tomorrow*? It was nonsense! You usually had to wait weeks, or months even, while people processed all your details and rubber-stamped all the forms and papers. But Gina didn't seem remotely concerned about this. Within minutes she was packing his few clothes and openly talking to Alice about what they could do with his bedroom. More pink, he guessed.

Late that night, Dax sat on the edge of his bed and surveyed the small suitcase that contained all his clothes and a few books and other belongings. Alice came in, in her nightie, and sat next to him. She didn't say anything for a while and it occurred to Dax, for the first time ever, that she *might* miss him.

'Mum says I can have this room, too, while you're gone,' said Alice.

'Fine,' said Dax. 'Paint it pink. I don't care.'

'Are you really a genius?'

'Don't be daft.'

'So why do they want you at this school?'

'Search me. I think it's a load of codswallop. But good for you, eh? Another pink room. Your dolls can live in it.'

Alice paused again and then said, quietly, 'I'll take them out. When you come back.' She stood up and looked at him for a moment. 'There's ointment in the bathroom, you know. For your cheek.' As she left, it struck Dax that she *was* the only one who'd noticed the bruise.

The next morning Dax put on his Bark's End Junior uniform for the last time. Would there be a uniform at Tre-wotsit college? Gina was edgy and excited at breakfast. She let him have as much milk as he wanted on his cereal (she normally threw a fit if he had more than a teaspoonful) and talked to him in a breathy, almost pleasant way. Dax guessed that she'd done some quick thinking and decided that if he *was* a genius, she might get to benefit from it in some way, so she should probably keep him sweet.

'Your dad said yes,' she told him. 'He thinks you should grab the opportunity. He says he'll come down to visit you there next month, to make sure everything's OK.' Dax nodded. He would have liked to talk to his father himself, but hadn't been offered the phone. On

51

the rare occasion when they *did* talk, Gina was always hovering nearby. She would snatch the phone away from him before he finished, claiming that the cost of calls to oil rigs in the North Sea was outrageous.

Dax walked to school early, to get away from Gina being weirdly nice. He felt unreal—rather as if it was the last day of the Christmas term, when nobody is expected to work and kids bring in games and fancy dress. It was his *last day*. Would he get the chance to see how Matthew and Toby were coping after yesterday? Would they even be there?

A removals lorry pulled up beside him as he walked dreamily down Woodside Lane. The cab door opened and a bearded man in a blue boiler suit jumped out. 'Hang on, son,' he said. And at first Dax thought he might be asking for directions. A second later he realized his mistake. As another man swiftly got out of the cab on the road side and opened the back door of the lorry, the bearded man expertly grabbed Dax and hauled him into the back of it. Dax took a lungful of air and prepared to shout, but before he could even squeak he was sprawling on the floor of the empty lorry container and the door was slammed shut behind him. The container was lit, and completely empty, except for one man, sitting cross-legged in the corner. It was Owen Hind.

Owen looked at him without smiling. 'Sorry, Dax,' he said, 'but I couldn't let you go back to school today. Not after yesterday.'

'What do you mean? What are you talking about?'

babbled Dax, extremely frightened. He turned and beat at the lorry doors, but they were secured sturdily from the outside. From somewhere towards the cab, Dax heard a radio being switched on and the volume turned up, loudly. To mask his shouts, he guessed. Dax faced Owen Hind again. He was still seated and calm. 'I knew you were a fake!' Dax shouted. 'I knew it!'

'No, Dax, I'm not,' said Owen Hind. 'And I'm sorry I'm going to have to put you through this, but it just has to be done.' He took a small notebook out of his pocket (he was no longer in the suit, but wearing a casual, green, thick-weave shirt, khaki jeans, and boots) and turned a pencil in his fingers. He didn't even look at Dax and showed no sign at all of coming towards him.

'Do it, Dax,' he said flatly. 'Change.'

Dax stared at him, too scared to speak.

'OK, then,' sighed Owen Hind, after a pause. 'Let's get this over and done with.'

Suddenly he thumped on the wall of the container, and a second later the truck's engine started. Panic flooded into Dax and again he turned and pounded on the lorry doors, shrieking and shouting. As the truck lurched and rolled on the uneven surface of the road, Dax was thrown sideways and pitched onto the floor. Lying there, he cast a scared look across at Owen who, still seated, was now holding a small glass bottle. He had put some kind of white mask on and was tipping drops of the bottle's contents onto the metal floor of the truck. Then he tucked the bottle back into his pocket, folded his arms, and looked calmly across at Dax over the top of the mask.

At this moment a thick vapour, with a choking smell, rose up from the drops he had spilled. It filled Dax with a sick dread and made his skin tingle. A cold feeling swam up through his nose and down into his lungs and the truck container began to spin around and around. He could hear his own heartbeat pulsing in his ears, getting faster and faster. 'Don't!' he heard himself sob. 'Stop it! I don't want to—' and then his vision clouded with grey and the grey turned to blue and the blue turned to black and then . . . nothing.

'God alive,' he heard Owen breathe. 'I'll never get used to this.'

Foggily, Dax raised his snout. Owen was sitting exactly where he'd been before, but his mask was pulled down and his face was ashen. The lorry had stopped and it was very quiet. Owen gazed back at him and there was no fear in his face; just a look of deep regret.

'Dax—I am truly sorry I had to do this. Are you OK?' He knelt up and held out his hand. Dax *should* have attacked him. Yet he didn't. Owen Hind *knew*. He had known even before. Maybe he could tell Dax what was going on, and even if he couldn't, the *relief* that somebody else knew was so great that Dax felt like laughing and crying all at once. He rose unsteadily, stretched his fox limbs, walked across to Owen, and then sat back on his haunches to return the man's fascinated gaze.

'Are you OK?' Owen said again, and closer, Dax could

see beads of sweat on his brow. It was reassuring. Dax nodded and curled his tail around his feet. 'I suppose you want to know what's going on,' said Owen. Dax nodded again. 'OK,' sighed Owen. 'I'll tell you as much as I know.'

He steepled his fingers together and shut his eyes for a moment and then opened them, with a determined, focused look. 'I wasn't lying,' he said. 'I do work for the government and the education department—but on a slightly unusual project. It's my job to find children like you as quickly as possible, and get them into the COLA Club. I think you may be the last one. You're the only one I've found in three months and they were coming through much faster before. You're one of our Children Of Limitless Ability, Dax—that's what COLA stands for. About eighteen months ago we started picking up on the first of them. Children doing extraordinary things . . . like healing with a touch, having startlingly accurate premonitionary dreams, telekinetic powers—being able to shift objects with their mind power—dowsing: that's finding stuff with mind power (sorry if you know about these things already, Dax—I know you can't really tell me); then glamourists—kids who can really conjure illusions—trick people into seeing what's not there—or others who just vanish, literally disappear or fade out of sight. And one—just one other—who could turn into an animal. But he didn't make it. He died before we could bring him in. Dax—I didn't want to waste any time with you. I *couldn't* lose another shapeshifter.

'So that's why I had to know as soon as possible,

and why I couldn't risk you going back to school after yesterday. If those two thugs had come out of their shock and worked out that it was you who'd attacked them, I wouldn't have fancied your chances. That's why I had to get you into a situation where the shift would happen. I absolutely loathe this part of it, but unfortunately, at this stage, the only way to bring about the shift is to put you into a state of extreme panic. If we'd just met up for a nice chat, you would have evaded all my questions and nothing would have happened, and COLA Club will *not* accept a student until there is no doubt that he or she *is* a COLA. So the stuff you inhaled was a concoction designed to bring about extreme terror and brief unconsciousness. It hasn't harmed you, and I hope you can forgive me for using it.'

Dax put his head on one side, clearly considering this. His snout dropped to study his tail and then he looked up at Owen and gave a curt little nod. Owen laughed and shook his head, marvelling at the boy fox.

'You know,' he said, with a slight shake in his voice, 'I have seen some amazing things in my life, but this really is astonishing. Anyway . . . to come back to today. Your school will be informed today that you won't be returning. Do you think your friend Clive is likely to tell anyone about what happened? Do you think he knows?' Dax shook his head, astounded that Owen knew so much. How *could* he? 'I know, I know,' Owen raised his hand. 'It must be very weird to hear all this, but trust me, I have some very special help in finding out things when it's urgent. I know that you followed your friend into the school basement, presumably because you saw him being chased down there, and I know that his attackers came running out two minutes later, screaming and bloodied and babbling about monsters and wolves. To be honest, I wasn't sure exactly what I would see when you changed. I'm quite relieved you're a fox. Foxes are usually tolerated when they're seen. You'd have had a harder time of it as a wolf.'

Dax made up his mind to ask Owen, as soon as he could, exactly *what* happened when he changed. He still had no idea about this process because he always seemed to lose consciousness. It was very frustrating.

'At COLA Club you'll be safe,' Owen continued. 'You'll be among your own kind, and you'll be taught how to control your power—as well as your usual schooling!' he added, with a laugh. 'Don't think you'll be getting out of *that*. You'll also be studied, by people like me who need to understand what's happening and why we've found so many COLAs these last two years—what it all means. You'll like Tregarren College, Dax; it's a great place.'

Owen paused and then said, 'That's really enough for now. I have a lot more to tell you, but it's not really fair when you can't talk back . . . can you?' he added, curiously.

Dax tried to say something. He tried to say, 'No—I don't think I can.' What came out was a series of small whines and rather comical growls. Dax shut his mouth and firmly shook his head and Owen roared with laughter. After a second or two, Dax couldn't help but join in, in a series of peculiar raspy barks. It must have made the most bizarre scene, he thought; a man and a fox in an empty lorry container, falling about laughing.

'Enough,' chortled Owen. 'You need to get home and get ready. We'll leave this evening. Now—you need to eat and you need to sleep.' He pulled a small knapsack out from the corner behind him. In it were a shallow metal bowl, a flask, and a paper packet. He undid the flask and poured water into the bowl and Dax, realizing that he was in fact very thirsty, lapped it up quickly. Then Owen opened the packet to reveal some cooked sausages. They smelt delicious and Dax felt ravenous, but he held back, glancing uneasily from the food to Owen. 'It's OK,' said Owen. 'There's nothing in them, I promise. Just top quality pork. I cooked them myself first thing this morning. Once you've eaten you'll want to sleep. Isn't that so? It's the animal way. You'll be off in no time, and then, I'm guessing, you'll be waking up as a boy and we can get you home.'

Dax ate the sausages inside a minute. They tasted wonderful to his fox tongue. Like his sight, hearing, and smell, Dax's sense of taste seemed to magnify ten times whenever he was a fox. As soon as they were gone, Dax curled up on the flat metal bed of the truck. It wasn't the most comfortable of sleeping places but already, in the wake of all the shock and fear and turmoil he'd been through, he found sleep stealing across him like a warm mist. How he could come to trust Owen so quickly after

what had happened he didn't know, but his instincts told
him he was completely safe. And so sleep came, and with
it came the change.

7

Owen and his two colleagues in the lorry dropped him off a couple of roads away from his home. 'All right, lad?' the bearded man had checked, anxiously, clearly wondering if there were any hard feelings. He *had* recently kidnapped the boy, after all. 'We wouldn't have hurt you, son,' he added, glancing at the well-built driver. 'Minding government ministers is our usual line of work.'

'I'm fine,' said Dax, with a cheery smile. And he *was* fine. He felt fantastic. Owen had left him to sleep for a couple of hours and he had woken up as a boy, but he seemed to have retained some of the energy and vitality he felt as a fox. He was also hugely excited now about COLA Club.

'I'll collect you at about six,' called Owen. 'Be ready.'

'I will,' yelled Dax and happily turned to walk home. Home wouldn't be home to him for much longer, he thought. If it ever really had been. It was late morning and he guessed that Gina would be out shopping. He hoped so; the last thing he needed was a grilling from Gina about why he was home early. He'd prepared himself with a story that the school had let him off the afternoon lessons because it was his last day, but wasn't sure she'd swallow it. Owen had told him not to worry;

he'd arrange things at the school so there would be no trouble. His calm authority on this matter was slightly frightening—Dax didn't know anyone else who could claim to control a head teacher.

He turned into his road and made for the row of graceless houses where he lived and didn't notice, until it was too late, that someone was waiting, half-concealed by the rhododendron bush, in the front garden. So much for his fox instincts, he thought, as the young woman stood up from the side of his front doorstep where she'd been sitting, making him jump.

'Hello,' she said. 'I'm Caroline Fisher, from the *Messenger*.'

Dax stopped dead and stared at her. She was small, slim, and pretty with a neat blonde bob and wide grey eyes. She was wearing a short red dress, with a white cardigan, and looked the picture of innocence, with a large basket-weave bag over her shoulder and a notebook and pen in one hand. Dax wasn't fooled for a second.

'What are you doing here?' he asked.

'Waiting to talk to you,' she beamed. 'You *are* Dax Jones, aren't you?'

'What if I am?'

'Look,' she frowned slightly, concerned, and slightly nervous, 'I didn't mean to frighten you. I'm just a brand-new reporter and I actually haven't done this before.'

Like heck, thought Dax, although he admired the effort.

'My editor sent me down here to find out something

about a strange attack on two of your fellow pupils at Bark's End Junior School,' she said and then bit her lip and shuffled on the doorstep. It was award-winning stuff, thought Dax. She raised her big grey eyes to his and gave him an endearing, hopeful smile. 'Can I come in?' she asked. 'It's a bit awkward standing around where the neighbours can hear.'

'Hear what?' asked Dax, coldly.

She looked at him hard and realized that the act wasn't working. She straightened her back, lifted her chin, and said, in a cool—*warning*—voice, 'About a boy who turns into a raging wild animal when provoked.'

Dax stared at her, aghast. How much did she know? Who had been talking to her? He didn't speak.

'I'm sorry, didn't you hear me?' she said, suddenly, with a gleam in her eyes. 'Do I need to say it LOUDER? ARE YOU THE BOY WHO—?'

'Shut up!' said Dax, angrily. He fumbled with his front-door key and let them both in as quickly as he could, his heart racing. How was he going to deal with this? What could he do? He wished heartily that Owen had come back with him. He'd have had this reporter *neutralized* or something.

As soon as he'd closed the hallway door she started, notebook open and pen poised. 'OK, Dax, we both know that something pretty weird happened at your school yesterday and it seems that *you* were right in the middle of it.'

'I really don't know what you're talking about,' said

Dax, through gritted teeth. He even wished that Gina was home now—she would have seen the girl off in no time. Except, of course, that she would have wanted to know *why* a reporter was here in the first place.

Caroline Fisher sighed and sat down on the stairs, resting her notebook on her knee. 'All right, Dax—if you don't know what I'm talking about, why were you so keen to let me in when I started shouting?'

He said nothing, but looked at her mutinously. He *had* to think of a way to get rid of her.

'Fine. Don't talk. I'll tell you what *I* know,' she said, with a smirk. 'Around lunchtime yesterday, two boys at Bark's End Junior School were seen running down the corridor, covered in blood and scratches, screaming about a monster—a dog or a wolf—which had attacked them in the basement.

'Apparently, they'd been down there larking around with another pupil and having a bit of a laugh with him—and by the way, Dax, I *know* what it means when two well-built lads have a *bit of a laugh* with one small, swotty kid—and then the swotty kid's friend turns up to try to help. And then, there's a bit more *larking around* and all of a sudden there's a wild thing attacking the two big lads and the swotty kid's friend has disappeared.'

Dax sank down against the hallway wall. He stared at his hands.

'So anyway; there's a bunch of kids in the corridor who *swear blind* that only one pupil came back out of the basement door after the first two ran out, and he just

63

went straight to the school toilets, refusing to speak to anyone, and then back to class. Nobody saw anyone or any*thing* come out after that—and these kids say they stayed put, because they wanted to find out what was going on. The caretaker and the year head came back to search the basement and there was nothing there. So what do you think, Dax? What could have happened to the fourth boy and this wild animal?'

Dax looked at Caroline Fisher. 'I think you'll write whatever you like, whatever *I* say,' he said, as calmly as he could.

'But wouldn't it be better if I could write the truth?' she said, earnestly, leaning forward on the step and scanning his face for clues.

Dax tried another gambit. 'OK,' he said, in a voice heavy with sarcasm, 'I found my mate getting beaten up so I magicked myself into a wild dog and bit Toby's and Matthew's bums. Will that do?'

The reporter compressed her lips and breathed sharply through her nose.

'Because, honestly—that's exactly what happened,' went on Dax, sensing he was winning. 'And now, if you don't mind, I've got some packing to do.' Damn! As soon as he'd said it, he knew it was a mistake.

'Packing?' she said, quickly. 'Where are you going?'

'It's none of your business,' he said and opened the front door. 'You really do have to go. And look . . . ' He paused, searching for the right words and tone, and hoping for the best. 'If you really *are* a brand-new reporter, don't you think that writing stories about mysterious wild animals in schools is a bit of a wobbly start? Nobody will take you seriously—will they?'

Caroline walked outside and turned on the step. She looked at Dax keenly, her head tilted to one side. 'Won't they?' she said. And then she left.

Clive's house was a nice semi-detached place with a pleasing brick arch over the porch. A sprawling buddleia hedge occupied most of the small front garden and inside this, Dax waited in the late afternoon sun. The leaves tickled the back of his neck and he was desperate to get out and go home. Owen would be collecting him in a little over two hours and he couldn't wait to go.

But first he had to talk to his friend. Eventually he heard some vague and tuneless humming and knew Clive was back. Clive often hummed strange little tunes while he thought his clever thoughts. It was another one of the many things that marked him out for regular bully attention.

Dax stepped out of the bush as Clive opened his gate. The boy jumped violently and stood rigid, his hands gripping the little wrought-iron curls. Dax bit his lip. He hated to think that Clive was scared of him.

'I needed to see you, before I went,' he explained. Clive nodded, looking anxious. He didn't even ask *where* Dax was going. 'Clive—what's the matter? It's *me.*'

'I know it's you,' said Clive, quietly. 'And I know what you are. I just don't know what *kind* you are.'

'What are you *talking* about?' said Dax, impatiently. 'Look, I really haven't got much time, but there's stuff you need to know. What—what do you mean, you don't know what *kind* I am?'

Clive pushed the gate shut and went to the front step of his porch. He sat down heavily, dumping his satchel at his feet, and looked up at Dax. 'You might as well sit down,' he said, but he was clearly not very comfortable with the idea. Dax sat beside him and he shuffled away slightly. 'After I got home yesterday I got on the Internet and looked it up,' said Clive. 'There's a lot of rubbish, of course. A lot of stupid kids doing fantasy role-play games and stuff—but there's some proper legend there as well, about shapeshifters.'

'Shapeshifters?' echoed Dax. He was intrigued. He liked that name. He now remembered Owen using it in the lorry, earlier.

'Or skin-walkers, if you're the Navajo Indian type. But that doesn't seem likely. I mean, your mum came from Bangladesh, didn't she?'

'No—*her* mum did,' corrected Dax. 'But what about skin-walkers? What are you on about, Clive?'

'I hope you're *not* a skin-walker, Dax,' said Clive. He had picked up a buddleia twig and was twisting it nervously in his fingers until the green threads of its innards were visible. 'That would mean you were pretty bad. I think I'll like it better if you're a shaman.'

'I'm not any of these things!' protested Dax. 'I honestly don't know what you're talking about, Clive.'

Clive shifted and looked at him hard. 'If you can change into a fox, then you are a shapeshifter. There's no doubt about that.' So Clive knew. Clive had *not* explained it all away rationally as he had expected.

'I never thought you'd believe in stuff like that,' said Dax.

'Nor did I,' said Clive. 'But seeing is believing. When you fell behind the boiler you were a boy. And when you got up again, you were a fox.' He gulped and turned to look at Dax, hard. 'I—I don't think you're evil, Dax. I still don't know what kind you are; there are more kinds that I haven't had time to find out about. But if you keep doing it, you'll be in a lot of danger. If someone *else* sees you . . . '

'It's all right, Clive,' said Dax. 'Like I said, I'm going away. Somewhere safe. You don't have to worry. But I'm sorry I won't see much of you any more.'

Clive was still mashing his twig. 'I'm sorry too, Dax,' he said and his voice sounded bleak.

'But look,' said Dax, remembering Caroline Fisher, 'if anyone from the *Messenger* comes, you've got to say *nothing*, OK?'

'The *Messenger*? Have you had a reporter round?'

'Yes—and she had a lot of information already, about what other kids saw in the corridor, and she was really hard to get rid of. Her name's Caroline Fisher. She's blonde and pretty and a real pain. So look out.'

Clive nodded. 'OK. Thanks for letting me know.' He stood up and offered his small hand, stained with green from the mashed twig, for Dax to shake. It was an odd gesture from someone you'd known since you were five. For the first and only time, Dax felt a pang of regret. He *would* miss Clive. He shook Clive's hand solemnly.

'Will you be OK, without me to bite Toby and Matthew for you?' he asked, with a small grin.

'Yeah,' said Clive, grinning back. 'I'm going to tell them I conjured up a skin-walker and give them all the gory details of what'll happen *next* time they have a go at me. That's if they ever come back. Someone said today that Matthew's been sucking his thumb in front of toddlers' TV all day today. I *like* that idea.'

The boys laughed and the sound rose into the still afternoon air; natural and good. A world away from Navajo skin-walkers and shamans and danger. Dax turned to go. 'I can write to you,' said Clive, behind him. 'If you want.'

Dax turned again and nodded. 'As soon as I've got an address, I'll let you know.'

He got back home to find Gina and Alice waiting for him. He was stunned to see that Gina had bought a cake. It was covered in thick blue icing and had 'Good Luck Dax' piped across it in white. They shared the cake at teatime, although Dax was so excited that he couldn't eat much. Even Gina's weird pleasantness wasn't really getting through to him. He felt as if he had already gone, and being here still was like being a ghost. When the doorbell went, finally, at six o'clock and Owen appeared, Dax was deluged with relief and had to fight the urge to run out to the car and dive in, before anyone could change their mind. For years he'd been ending every single day with a climb up the stairs to his dank little bedroom. The idea of going back there this evening, even to nod goodbye at it as some people do when they leave a place, was absolutely appalling to him. Out! Out! He had to go!

He accepted a kiss and a hug from Gina. He was well practised at looking as if this was natural. It was an act he and Gina shared every Christmas, when family were there. Alice surprised him by taking his hand and giving it a bit of a squeeze as she said goodbye. It hadn't even occurred to Dax that he'd miss Alice, and even now he was pretty sure he wouldn't. But he did feel an odd sense of protectiveness towards her. He hoped she wouldn't take too much after Gina, left solely in her mother's company.

He chucked his small case into the back of Owen's Jeep and climbed in at the front. Owen looked at him as he turned the key in the ignition. 'Ready?' he said. Dax smiled a wide and glorious smile and settled back into his seat.

'Oh yes,' he said.

8

It was one of the most exciting journeys of Dax's life. His very blood felt hot in his veins. He had *left* home; left Gina and Alice behind and he was going somewhere completely new. Dax felt as if he was *fizzing*. Energy coursed through him and he had to tap his feet and wiggle his fingers just to let some of it out. The feeling was so extreme that at one point he got a little panicky. What if this made him turn into a fox?

'Owen . . .' he asked. The man had been driving in a comfortable silence since their departure and had only spoken to him once or twice. He looked round and grinned at the state Dax was in. 'Could I—could I turn into a fox, when I'm like this?' said Dax.

'I don't think so, Dax. Not unless you really, really want to. And maybe not then. Not yet.'

'But how do you know? I might just go pop and do the furry thing at any time. It could happen, you know, down at the shops or on the bus. How do you know?'

'I've researched, Dax, and know a bit about shapeshifters. Although you're not really typical. Most reports of shapeshifters come from the Navajo Indians and in the case of these people the shifting is usually very deliberate and often brought about with the use of drugs.

It's not generally for the greater good, either. Shifters among Native Americans are very much feared. They're said to lead people into harming themselves, even killing themselves. If you revealed what you were among *that* community you'd be dead inside a day.'

Dax gulped. 'Are you talking about skin-walkers?'

Owen looked round, impressed, before fixing his eyes back on the dark road. 'You've been doing some homework!'

'No, my friend Clive did. He looked it up on the Net.'

'Clive? You've been talking to *Clive*?'

Dax was alarmed. Idiot! He hadn't meant to tell on Clive to anyone. What if they sent someone round to . . . to neutralize him or something? Dax peered across at Owen, wretchedly. In spite of his strong instinct to like and trust the man, he had met him only yesterday and since then Owen had—*ahem*—kidnapped and drugged him!

'Yes. He worked it out. But he won't tell anyone, Owen. He won't. He's much too bright to do something like that. He . . . '

'Relax, will you?' said Owen. 'What do you think I'm going to do? Have him shot?'

Dax said nothing. He felt foolish and yet he also felt that, if it were important enough, Owen might well have people shot.

As if he was reading Dax's mind, Owen said, gently, 'Look, Dax, I know we got off to a pretty weird start back there, but I'm really not a violent man. I won't tell you that everyone you meet at COLA Club is good and innocent—they're not—but we don't go around bumping people off. The fact is, we can't possibly keep *everything* a secret. We've got a hundred and eight—well, a hundred and nine now—students at the college and there's no way we could keep their special powers from their families and some of their friends. There are police chiefs, nurses, head teachers (yes, really), and all kinds of ordinary people who know *something* about our students. Naturally, we keep it as low key as possible, and there are rules that you'll have to follow to help with that, but we have to rely on people's good sense and, so far, we've managed.

'People in the community around Tregarren College know that it's a place for especially gifted kids and, of course, rumours occasionally get out, but generally nobody bothers us. The Cornish are remarkably unfazed about supernatural stuff anyway. Remember, a lot of them still believe in Knockers.'

'Knockers?' echoed Dax.

'Spirits that live down in the tin mines.'

'And are there such things?'

Owen smiled, but simply said, 'Clive will be fine, Dax. He's a very intelligent boy and he hasn't got many mates who he'll want to talk to about this anyway. Stay in touch with him. It's good to have a strong anchor in the normal world.'

Dax wanted to ask him how he knew that much about Clive, but guessed it was the same way he'd known about *him*. He'd have to ask about that later, but now he realized there was something else he needed to say to Owen. Urgently.

'OK. Clive said he'd write anyway. But, Owen, what about the reporter?'

Owen choked and swerved the car over to the side of the road and stopped the engine. He turned to stare urgently at Dax. 'Reporter?' he demanded. '*What* reporter, Dax? Tell me everything.' Dax told him about Caroline Fisher and how she'd forced her way into the house to talk to him. How he'd just been sarcastic at her and told her nothing, really.

'I'm not stupid, you know,' he said, defensively. 'I didn't say anything and I just, kind of, made fun of her.'

Owen clapped his hands over his eyes and groaned. 'Oh, great. Make fun of the reporter. Eeesh! Dax—little word of advice. Be stupid, be chatty, be sad, pretend you're Greek or a deaf mute, but *never* make fun of reporters. It's a red rag to a bull. What was her name?'

'Caroline Fisher. From the *Messenger*.'

Owen nodded. He stared into space for a moment and then switched the engine on. 'OK, Dax. Don't worry. I won't have her encased in concrete and thrown in the river—although if ever I came close to it, it would be for a reporter. Well done for not telling her anything.'

Dax wriggled uncomfortably in his seat and Owen snapped around to him again, immediately. 'What? What else did you say, Dax?'

'Only that—well—I sort of said I had to go and pack. And she wanted to know where I was going, and . . . '

'You didn't tell her . . . '

'No—of course not. That's when I made her leave. I didn't say *anything* else at all.'

Owen shook his head and shifted the car into gear. 'OK,' he said, levelly. 'Anything else I should know?'

'No,' said Dax, and the two were quiet for many miles. Eventually, when the evening was late and very dark, Dax began to make out the jagged coastline of Cornwall and the smell he'd been picking up since Devon was sharp and wonderful in his nose. Salty and metallic and richly earthy. They drove down unlit winding lanes with high banks of wild grass on either side, and a few late insects chirruped and ticked in a soft chorus through the open slice of his window.

Dax broke the silence in the car with the thought that had been troubling him since his last talk with Clive. 'Owen—this shapeshifting thing. Is it—evil?'

Owen sighed. 'Look, Dax, *powers* in themselves aren't evil. It's the person who has them that decides. One thing I can tell you for sure, Dax, is that you're *not* completely good. Nor am I. I don't set out to harm anyone, but I know that I *could*. It's right there inside me, and it's inside you, too. Believe it, Dax,' he said, as Dax frowned defensively, 'because it's part of what will help you to survive.'

Dax was beginning to feel sleepy. He'd have been in bed by now, back at home in his narrow little room. He shivered at the thought and Owen reached across to the back seat and handed him a fleecy jacket. 'Try to get some sleep,' he said. 'We've got about an hour and half's driving left and you could use some.' Dax bunched the jacket up into a pillow, pulling the sleeves around his neck like a scarf, and settled into the corner of the seat. He didn't think he could, but soon he was drifting down through the layers of sleep, although always aware of the note of the car engine as Owen changed up and down through the gears around the narrow, winding lanes, and the occasional clicking of the indicator before they turned.

He must have fallen deeper than that because, abruptly, it seemed, the interior car light was on, and Owen was shaking him gently by the shoulder. 'Dax. Dax, wake up. We're here.'

Dax sat up quickly, dazed and disorientated. Then he heard the sound of the sea and excitement flooded through him, so that his hands shook as he undid his seatbelt. Shrugging himself into the fleece he climbed out of the car into a steady, cold breeze as Owen took his case from the back. Dax was puzzled. He turned fully round, but all he could see was what appeared to be a huge stone chimney, rising up into the dark sky from a base of rocky, uneven ground. A dim light was shining from a window at the base of the chimney and, as he watched, Dax saw the door next to it open, sending a bigger shaft of light across the stony ground, as a man with a torch and a dog at his heels came out to meet them.

'Ho, Owen!' he called. 'You've brought Dax Jones, I see.'

Dax felt odd, hearing his name from this stranger with his Cornish accent and his dog. The dog—a shaggy, curly brown thing that came up to its master's hips—walked towards him and sniffed at him. Then it sat back suddenly, unsteadily, on its haunches and gave Dax what can only be described as a *hard stare*. Dax crouched down. He didn't attempt to pet the dog, because it didn't seem appropriate. This dog *knew*. Dax looked steadily into its eyes, as they reflected back at him, red discs in the torchlight, and then the dog stood and walked towards him until its cold wet nose met his. Dax smiled, delightedly. It likes me! he thought. It thinks I'm OK!

'Well, if Barber takes to you, you must be all right,' said the man, warmly. He was in his sixties and wearing a sort of dark uniform, like a doorman's. He had a short grey beard and looked like an old sea captain.

'This is Mr Pengalleon, our gatekeeper,' said Owen, depositing Dax's case on the ground, so he could clap the man warmly on the shoulder. 'And this is Barber, our gate dog. He has possibly the loudest bark in the South-West Peninsular. Funny that he didn't bark at Dax, eh?' he said to Mr Pengalleon.

'Barber knows what he knows,' said Mr Pengalleon, sagely. 'Now get this boy in. Wind could freeze him to the ground tonight.'

Owen picked up the case again and steered Dax towards the great chimney. 'But where's the college?' Dax murmured. 'There's nothing here.' Owen grinned as they stepped into the gatekeeper's warm room. It was perfectly circular, with white painted brick walls, dark oak planks across the floor, and three doors leading off it. It smelt of old, sweet tobacco and housed an ancient desk and chair, placed by the window, a couch covered in blankets, where Barber was now curling up comfortably, and a high-backed, winged leather armchair by the fireplace which was filled with red coals and sending a glorious golden warmth across the room.

'Keep moving,' said Owen and propelled Dax across the round room and out of one of the doors.

'But where—?' asked Dax again and then he stopped. The door had opened back on to the night sky and the stars shone down upon a scene so totally unexpected that Dax simply gaped. They were perched on the edge of a dramatic drop. A thick stone wall prevented them from falling to oblivion and two hundred metres below it Dax could see the churning cauldron of the Cornish sea, hurling itself against the dark rocks. But to his right, a narrow stone path which slid into rough-cut steps from time to time, wound down a craggy, gently sloping cliff face. The lights were what struck Dax most. Chains and chains of tiny white orbs hung along the path, swinging in the wind. They zigzagged up and down a path which wove past a series of stone buildings that might have grown from the rock and soil and grass that surrounded them. Many of them were curved and had chimneys in their conical, dark grey slate roofs, which shone blue in the light from the tiny orbs and the stars overhead.

On a plateau halfway between the top of the cliff and

the sea was a huge jutting promontory of flat rock, upon which was a long, low, stone building. It had clearly been put there in more recent years, because it was a purpose-built college, with a sort of open ended quadrangle containing a neat square lawn which had a square pond and a fountain at the centre, and many high, sparkling windows. Dax was entranced. He had never imagined anything like this.

Owen led him down the path and its crops of steps, past the small curved dwellings, some of which showed soft lights through the old, eddied glass of their windows, along a straight stretch which had Owen ducking, because it passed beneath a low rocky outcrop with a fringe of damp fern at the edge, then over a small arched wooden bridge spanning a stream, which hurried through a shallow, water-carved bed in the rock before throwing itself gleefully into a waterfall and out of sight.

They walked past the college building and Dax could feel that the rock beneath his feet had been hewn flat by man, to accommodate the building and its grounds. Skirting another turn in the cliff face, Dax saw a second promontory pointing out to sea, lower down, rising steeply perhaps seven metres above the water. It was fenced with stout wooden posts and timber and completely turfed over to create a sports ground. Dax could just make out the markings of a football pitch. Kick one over *that* fence and you wouldn't get your ball back in a hurry, he thought.

'Like it?' asked Owen, beaming proudly. 'There's a lido too, just beyond the pitch. You can't see it from here.'

'What's a lido?' asked Dax, intrigued.

'An outdoor swimming pool. This one's natural, fed by the sea. There was already an almost complete circle of rocks, creating a little calm swimming area, and the college had more put into place to secure it totally. It's still tidal, of course, because there are plenty of gaps in the rocks, but it's safe to swim in. Cold. But safe. Here we go.'

They had arrived at another stone building, this one set on a broad ledge of rock a little higher up the cliff than the main college, which could still be seen, just beneath an overhang of rock which reached out to sea like half an arch, as if expecting another outstretched span of rock to meet it. Dax stared up, craning his neck, but couldn't see the top of the cliff. The students' living and sleeping hall was built of the same soft grey stone as the college, and had the same steeply pitched slate roof. Inside it was warm and lined with golden wood. The floor was tiled with the local stone and a long corridor, with opaque glass doors leading off on either side, led to a lofty sitting room at the far end of the building. It was dimly lit by one lamp and the last few red embers in the open stone grate. In one corner of the sitting area a spiral staircase rose and up this Owen led Dax.

'You're in the end dorm,' said Owen, quietly. 'We'll have to keep the noise down because the other boys will be asleep. You're in with Gideon and Barry. You've got the best dorm, I think.'

He pushed open the door and Dax saw a long room

with a low, sloping ceiling. The wooden floor was covered, along the foot of the beds, by a thick, warm run of green carpet and beside each bed was a sturdy oak trunk. Four chests of oak drawers faced the beds and a long wardrobe filled the end wall. 'We'll sort your stuff out in the morning. You should just get to bed now,' whispered Owen, putting Dax's case on the trunk next to one of the two empty beds. 'The bathroom's just opposite. I'll leave you now. See you in the morning.'

Dax wandered across to the white-tiled bathroom and washed and brushed his teeth. He was bone tired, but wished he could explore. Still, there's plenty of time, he told himself with a thrilled grin. He padded back into the dorm, where he could hear the rhythmic breathing of the two sleeping boys. He couldn't make out their faces. One was completely buried in his thick, blue quilt, making a muffled whistling sound when he breathed out, and the other had his back turned, although Dax could see that his fair hair was thick and wiry and tufting in all directions.

His bed was firm and warm and comfortable and the linen smelt faintly of lavender. Dax lay on his back and stared up at the stars through the window in the ceiling that slanted across the head end of his bed. He could hear the muffled thunder of wave upon wave hitting the coast and as his eyes began to close he felt that he had never, truly, been happier in his life.

9

'. . . don't. You know you're not supposed to. You'll get into trouble.'

'It's all right. I'm keeping it nice and steady. Nobody will know.'

'Sartre will pick it up! Hang on—is he waking up?'

'Nah. He's gonna sleep till next century, this one. What do you reckon he does?'

'Oi! Keep it *steady*. If you let it drop . . . It's too heavy!'

'It's not *that* heavy! I can manage it.'

Dax detected pride and a slight cockiness in the boy's voice as his ears gradually awoke. He furrowed his brow, his eyes still shut, and tried to work out where he was.

'Maybe he's another glamourist! That would be nice for you, wouldn't it?' The boy was teasing now.

'No, it wouldn't. But it would be great for *you* to get another telly!' Dax's face must have registered his confusion at these odd words because the same voice said, again, 'Careful, Gid! He *is* waking up.'

'I reckon he's just another medium. Bor-ing!' Gid, whoever *he* was, put on a high, wavery voice. 'Running Nose, my spirit guide, tells me that there will be fluctuations in the firmament and stirrings in the depths of the—the—school canteen gravy tin. Oh no! I see sausages! Many, many burnt sausages! Does this mean anything to you . . . ?'

Dax burst out laughing, opened his eyes, and was immediately hit in the face by a football. He sprang up and looked around him, confused and slightly panicked, his eyes watering. In a millisecond his brain had slotted him into COLA Club, and offered up a little collection of recent scenes that had led up to his being right here, getting hit in the face with a football. Both boys had scrambled back from the edge of his bed and were sitting on the next one, wearing pyjamas. They looked stricken, guilty and nervous. The ball bounced once and rolled away across the floor.

'Sorry, mate!' said the one whose voice marked him out as 'Gid'. 'You kind of startled me and I lost concentration.'

'And decided to chuck a football in my face?' said Dax, groggily, realizing that this was the blond, tufty-haired boy he'd seen last night. 'Nice to meet you too!'

'No, no—he didn't mean to,' said the other boy. He was tall and well built; a little podgy, with dark, close-cropped hair and worried grey eyes. 'He was just floating it over your head and then, well, when you laughed like that, he couldn't keep it *steady.*' This last he directed meaningfully at the other boy, with a glare. 'I *told* you not to!'

The tufty-haired boy suddenly beamed and held out his hand to Dax. 'I'm Gideon Reader. Telekinetic and top striker in the Tregarren Tigers.' Dax shook his hand and felt a grin build up on his face. Gideon was very fair, with blond eyelashes and brows setting off his pale green eyes, and a scattering of pale golden freckles across his nose. 'This, sitting *next* to me, is Barry Blake. He does glamour.' Dax had a momentary vision of the heavy-set Barry twirling on a small stage in a gold frock and a feather boa, then shook his head. No—glamour was . . . what was it Owen had told him?

'His *line* of glamour is disappearing,' explained Gideon, evidently realizing that Dax was new to all this. 'Although it's never very difficult to find him.'

'That's all *you* know!' said Barry, but he was grinning too, and looking at Dax speculatively. There was a pause, and both boys went on regarding him, apparently waiting for him to say something.

'Oh—sorry!' Dax swung his legs out of bed and sat opposite his new dorm-mates. 'I'm Dax Jones.'

They smiled and nodded. And waited. Dax stared back at them, beginning to feel embarrassed. It dawned on him that they were expecting him to tell them what he *did*. Dax didn't want to. Not yet. And in truth, he didn't really know what to say. 'I turn into a fox' just sounded so . . .

'Oh—we've got one of *those*.' Gideon flopped back on his bed with a groan and covered his eyes. 'It's another film star!'

'What do you mean?' said Dax, stung.

Gideon sprang up. He grabbed a towel from the top of his trunk, wrapped it around his shoulders and began to walk mincingly along the room. 'I'm sorry, but I simply *must* have my privacy,' he said in a breathy, American accent. 'Please—please—no press!' He pulled the towel over his head and the muffled voice continued, 'Please, I just want to be left *alone*!'

Dax couldn't help laughing, and Gideon pulled the towel off abruptly and hared back to sit down opposite him again, leaning forwards onto his knees and coaxing him determinedly. 'Come on, Dax Jones. Give! Are you a medium?'

'No,' Dax laughed. 'I'm a small.'

Gideon cackled and then resumed his forthright stare. 'You can't be a glamourist, because you didn't know what that meant. Are you another tele, like me?'

'No,' grinned Dax. Barry looked relieved.

'Snake charmer? Water dowser? Clairvoyant? Clairaudient? Illusionist? Alchemist?' Dax kept shaking his head, wondering if Gideon would guess right. 'Palm reader? Rune reader? Soothsayer? Seer? Healer? Astral projector? *Slide* projector? Photocopier? Fax machine . . . ?' Gideon tailed off, shaking his head.

'Give it up,' said Barry. 'He'll tell us when he wants to. Come on—you'd better get up and dressed, Dax, or there'll be no breakfast left.'

When Dax returned from the bathroom, both boys were out of their pyjamas, and changing into their day clothes. 'Yours'll be in the drawer,' said Gideon, shrugging into a turquoise sweatshirt with Tregarren College embroidered on to it in white. Barry wore the same, and they both had on jeans and trainers. 'This is weekend stuff,' explained Gideon as Dax pulled open the drawer nearest to him and found another neatly pressed and folded sweatshirt. 'Your weekday uniform will be in the wardrobe.' Dax's sweatshirt smelt new and his name was printed on the label inside it. He undid his small case and peeled out some creased jeans; his only pair. They looked OK with the sweatshirt. He hoped nobody would notice his scuffed and aged trainers. The sweatshirt fitted him perfectly.

As the three boys headed out of the room towards breakfast, Dax found himself saying, almost without thinking, 'Shapeshifter.'

Both boys stopped in their tracks. Barry stepped back a little and Gideon turned to look at Dax intently, and then let out a low whistle. 'Shapeshifter! Well . . . ' He ran his fingers swiftly through his messy hair and whistled again. 'And Owen put you in with *us*? Faaaantastic!' Before there was time to say more, a bell suddenly rang out. 'Quick!' said Gideon. 'We've only got five minutes to get to breakfast!'

The refectory was in the large college building that Dax had last seen awash with moonlight. Tregarren College was now gleaming in bright sunshine, teeming with other children and staff. A mild, salty breeze ruffled his hair as they walked down the stone steps from the dormitory building and along the path that led back under the rocky outcrop. The sea was calmer this morning, and reflecting a pearly blue sky.

Perhaps a hundred children were having breakfast, in a cacophony of chatter and clattering cutlery and crockery. They all seemed to be about Dax's age; some were wearing the same sweatshirt that he had on, and others were in their own clothes. It seemed that the sweatshirt was optional on a Saturday. There were, indeed, sausages on offer at the bright, blue-and-white-tiled school canteen, along with bacon and beans and eggs and mushrooms, being served by two cheerful, flushed ladies with Cornish accents. There were also racks and racks of breakfast cereals in large boxes, a dozen jugs of chilled fruit juices, milk, and water, and a warm corner where you could make toast and boil eggs for yourself. A huge urn of tea was steaming next to it. A dozen large round oak tables were arranged across the polished wooden floor of the refectory, with green leather-padded oak seats around them. To his left Dax could see a glorious vista of Cornish coast and sea through the tall arched windows that ran along one entire wall of the building.

He collected a plate of bacon, eggs, and mushrooms and a cup of hot brown tea and joined Gideon and Barry at a table near the windows. Several other children peered at him curiously as he sat down.

'So, then, Dax,' said Gideon, over a bowl of cornflakes. 'Tell us a bit more about this shapeshifting lark then. What's it like? When did it start? How long before Owen came for you?'

There were three other students at the table with them. Dax knew that they were *all* possessed of extraordinary powers, or they wouldn't be here, but he still didn't want to sit chatting about his own stuff just yet. 'I only found out a week ago,' he said quietly, sawing at his bacon.

Gideon paused and, to his credit, said, 'OK, mate. It's all a bit too new, I reckon. You don't have to say anything. I was majorly freaked out when mine started. One minute I was just normal, and the next, my dad was asking me to get the forks off the ceiling. Poor geezer thought the UFOs had landed.'

Dax was intrigued. 'What exactly do you do?' he asked.

'I can move things with my head. I mean—not by headbutting them, but—look—like this.' Gideon's face smoothed and a strange coolness stole across it, a *focus*. Dax felt his mouth fall open as the salt and pepper pots in the middle of the table rose six inches into the air, wobbling slightly, and then curved smoothly across the white tablecloth towards Barry's copious breakfast of bacon, sausages, beans, eggs, mushrooms, tomatoes, more eggs, and six triangles of buttered toast, before upending and scattering their contents onto his plate.

'Oi!' yelled Barry, not at all impressed. 'If I want seasoning I'll ask for it!' The salt and pepper pots dropped and rolled across the table and Gideon scooped them up and replaced them at the centre, looking around nervously.

'Gideon—you'll get us all into trouble,' said a girl opposite and Dax looked across at her and was immediately transfixed. She wasn't beautiful or even pretty, with a pale face and unremarkable brown hair, cut into a short bob, although her eyes were a violet blue and fringed with very thick, dark lashes. She looked about twelve but there was something somehow much *older* about her. Not in a creaky, aged sort of way, but as if those eyes had seen far more than you could possibly fit into twelve years. More than anything, though, Dax was entranced by her *voice*. It was low and soft and made him think of pebbles shifting in water. It was the loveliest, most calming voice he'd ever heard. Dax didn't realize he was staring until Gideon elbowed him hard in the ribs.

'Get over it, mate,' he said. 'It happens to all of us.'

'Wha—what do you mean?' stuttered Dax, blushing furiously.

'That's Mia. She can't help it. She makes everyone feel like that. It's her thing.'

'Her thing?'

'Yep. She's a healer. I'll show you.' Without warning, Gideon grabbed Dax's arm and gave it a wrist burn, twisting his skin in two directions until Dax shouted out. Then he dragged Dax round to Mia's side of the table and presented his red and stinging wrist to her. 'Go on, girl!' he challenged.

'Gideon, that's so childish,' she said, giving him a sharp glare, but taking hold of Dax's wrist without even looking. Her hands were cool and smooth and almost at once his skin began to tingle. He felt a wave of warmth build in her palms and cross into his skin like liquid and then the pain was completely gone. Dax could only stare at her, dumbfounded. Gideon reached over his shoulder and helped him to shut his mouth.

'Sorry about your dorm-mate,' said Mia, smiling at Dax.

Dax returned to his seat in a daze. 'It's all right,' said Gideon. 'You'll get used to her soon and it won't have such a strong effect. If it didn't wear off a bit she'd have the whole school following her around. Ah—here we go, Dax. That's what I meant by a film star!'

He was pointing to another girl, who had just collected her breakfast and was sitting as far as possible from the rest of the students. She had long blonde hair, fashionably layered, and was wearing embroidered jeans and a fluffy yellow top. Her fingernails were perfectly polished and the little zip-up clutch bag she carried matched the colour of her top perfectly. She looked, thought Dax, like something out of a television advert for washing powder or fizzy drinks, except that she wasn't smiling and studiously avoided looking anywhere but out of the window. She had a pretty face, but it looked closed and sulky.

'Lisa Hardman,' said Gideon, in a low voice. 'Absolute film star. Won't talk to anyone except a couple of girls in her dorm—sometimes. Can't stand it here apparently. Unlike most of us, she had a *life* back home before she came here. Very well-off dad. Nice house. Pony. Swimming pool and shopping trips to New York and stuff.'

'What's *her* thing?' asked Dax.

'Don't know yet. She's only been here two weeks and she won't tell anyone. Nobody has to tell, although it always gets out in the end, so it's probably easier to just get it over and done with. Anyway, she's desperate to go home and keeps phoning and writing to her dad. *My* dad would think I was barmy if I said I wanted to leave here. He thinks it's fantastic. Said he'd move in tomorrow if they let him.'

'So would mine,' said Barry. 'He wants one of the cobs up the cliff.'

Something strange occurred to Dax. He counted three, in total. Three references to just *one* parent. 'What about your mum?' he asked, slowly.

Gideon and Barry looked at each other for a moment, and then back at Dax. Gideon said, 'What about *yours*?'

Dax put down his knife and fork and said, in the usual understated way that he always tried to, 'Oh—I haven't got one. Well, I've got a stepmother, but my real mum died years ago.'

He waited for the shocked response. The older people were, the harder they seemed to take it, but even his own age often stumbled, blushed, didn't know what to say. Yet Barry just shrugged and went on with his immense breakfast and Gideon was actually grinning in a wry sort of way.

'So, then, you're definitely a COLA,' he said. Dax peered at him hard, trying to work out what he meant, and then Gideon stood up, saying to Dax, 'OK—stand by. A little roll call.' He cupped his hands in a megaphone around his mouth and shouted out: 'PEOPLE! Excuse me one moment, but for the benefit of Mr Jones, who's new, can we please have a dead mother hand-count?'

Dax was stunned. Hurt. He'd really started to like Gideon, in spite of the football in the face and the wrist burn, and now the boy was just making fun of him—and over the hardest thing in his life. But as he shot a venomous look at Gideon he realized that the hall had quietened, although a few students were making weary and irritated noises. Dax rose to his feet and let his eyes travel from one end of the room to the other. He felt cold. As far as he could see, every single child in the room had raised a hand.

10

Someone touched Dax's shoulder and he jumped violently and spun round. It was Owen, who was giving Gideon a warning look. 'Nice, Gideon,' he said drily. 'Very nice.' Gideon looked a little guilty and stared at his sausages. 'Sorry, Dax, have you finished your breakfast yet?' asked Owen. Dax nodded; there was plenty of it left but his appetite had just winked out. 'The principal would like to meet you—and his deputy. And then Gideon can show you around properly, unless you've had enough of him for one morning.'

He shot another glare at the boy and Gideon mumbled, 'Look—I was just trying to make him feel better. That he's not the only one. Sorry, Mr Hind. I didn't think he'd get all . . . all . . .'

'I'm not all *anything*!' protested Dax. 'I'm fine. And yes, I'd like him to show me around.' Gideon smiled up at him brightly.

'OK,' said Owen. 'Gideon, come over to the principal's office when you've finished breakfast. You'll need these.' He handed the boy two green printed slips and Gideon nodded and tucked them in his pocket.

As they walked across the neat square of grass in the quadrangle, Dax said, 'Is it true? Are we really all the same—all without our real mothers?'

'Bizarre, isn't it?' said Owen. 'It's one of the things we noticed pretty quickly. There's not one student here whose mother lived for more than four years after they were born. It seems a pretty brutal price for all the incredible talent we've discovered, but there it is.'

'What did they all die of?' asked Dax, remembering that his mother's death had been put down to heart failure—one of those sudden things that nobody expects in someone so young.

'A lot of natural causes,' said Owen, pushing open a door at the opposite corner of the quad and leading him into a conservatory area with tall parlour palms in pots and an aquarium filled with small silver sharks. 'Some were heart attacks, some strokes . . . they were all very quick.'

'What else is there? What else connects us all—apart from being around the same age?'

'Well, we're finding out more all the time, but one of the other chief connections is the weather.'

'The *weather*?'

'Yes. Did your dad ever mention what the weather was like during your birth or close to it?'

'Yes—yes he did!' said Dax, fascinated. 'He always told me that there was an incredible storm on the night I was born—and in the morning there was a blood-red sunrise and a really hot day.'

Owen nodded. 'Yes. It's usually something like that. Extreme heatwaves, strong electrical storm activity, double haloes around the sun; one even got a localized blizzard—in July. Anyway—here we are.' He knocked on a green painted door with a brass plate which read *Principal Wood*. A voice said 'Come!' and they went in.

The principal's office was lined with books, from floor to ceiling, on three walls, except where the endless leather tomes had been forced to arch around a small stone fireplace. The fourth wall was taken up with a tall window, framing another stunning view of the sea and the large grassy sports area, which jutted out into it. Owen motioned Dax to sit down on a blue leather sofa and then went over to lean against the window, his arms folded.

Dax regarded the two people sitting opposite him. Behind a long oak desk, his arms raised and his hands tucked at the back of his head, tilting easily back in his chair, was a man whose dark brown eyes were glittering with fascination. He was not a handsome man. In fact, thought Dax, he looked like a slightly damaged Siamese cat, with a thin, rather battered-looking face and a very slight cross to his eyes. He was lean and wiry and his brown hair flopped over his forehead in a boyish way, although he must have been in his forties. But in spite of his lack of looks, there was something very—Dax struggled for the word—very *charismatic* about him. You looked at him, and then looked some more, like it or not.

'Dax Jones,' he said, smiling deeply, as if he were about to tell a joke. 'Dax Jones. I'm Principal Wood. I'm very pleased to meet you. Let me introduce my deputy to you—Mrs Sartre.'

The woman next to him rose, walked across, and extended a graceful hand towards Dax and he half got up to take it. She was older than the principal and very elegant. Dressed in soft, dark-grey folds of wool, with a glittering amber stone on a chain around her throat, her pale auburn hair was swept into a low knot at the base of her neck, and her fine complexion was gently lined with the kind of furrows that suggested she had laughed, smiled, and cried a lot in her life. Behind round spectacles, her grey eyes scanned Dax thoroughly and, as he took her hand in a polite shake, there was a click of static and he felt a small shock pass up his arm. Mrs Sartre didn't let go of him—she squeezed his hand for some seconds and frowned slightly in concentration. When she *did* let him go, Dax dropped back into his seat with a thud, feeling slightly odd.

'Very much, Patrick,' she said—although, with a French accent, she said it as *Patreek*. 'Much, much more than I was expecting. How long has it been, now?'

'Just a matter of days,' said Principal Wood, glancing from his deputy to Dax and back again.

'Days . . .' she repeated, staring at Dax curiously. 'That is a very steep curve. I am a little worried. Has he any control?' This she directed at Owen.

'Not yet,' he said from the window. 'I had to use the Triple Eight. But when it happens it's fast and it's quite total. Unmistakable.'

'And what form do you take, Dax Jones?' said Mrs Sartre, now smiling at him.

'A . . . a fox,' he said, self-consciously.

'When you get angry, or scared, yes?'

'Yes—I think so.'

'Hmmm.' She walked to the door, deep in thought. She leaned her back against it, pressing her fingers to her temples briefly and then looking at him contemplatively once more. The principal and Owen seemed to be watching her closely, waiting for something.

'What concerns me most,' she said, 'is how angry you have been and how you have collected that anger—*here*.' She tapped the area just below her heart, in the centre of the ribcage. 'Here it builds and builds and then . . . goes cold.' Dax was startled. She was describing his volcano. The thing inside him that he'd had to cap and squash down for half his life. 'You think your angers have gone,' went on Mrs Sartre, walking across to him and touching his hair, which crackled slightly and began to rise to her fingers as if her hand was a charged balloon, 'but they have not. You carry them always. This is not good.'

Dax felt disappointed. He didn't know what he was supposed to say. Mrs Sartre sat down next to Principal Wood again.

'It's all right, Dax,' said the principal, warmly, and again Dax felt the man's charm wash over him. 'You don't need to worry. While you are here with us, we will help you to learn to control your shapeshifting powers. By the end of this term I expect you will have learned to change into a fox at will, rather than whenever you get scared or angry. You may even have got to grips with how to change *back* when you want—although I'm told that's harder. What we do here is allow our students to continue their education in safety and in the company of other children like them, who understand the particular difficulties of being so *different*. I'm sure that Mr Hind will have explained to you that we aim to be discreet about what happens here, for obvious reasons. Because some very *odd* things happen here. And some quite wonderful things happen here too. Dax,' he leaned forward on his desk, beaming, 'I'm so glad we found you. We thought we might never get another shapeshifter.'

He nodded, still smiling, at Owen, and Owen indicated to Dax that it was time to go. He rose and had begun to walk back across the principal's study when two strange things happened. The first was that, in a sudden sharp draught, Dax could *smell* something weird. He'd last scented it in the corridor back at his old school. It was unmistakably *fear*. He stopped in his tracks and at that same moment Mrs Sartre let out a small cry. She was staring straight at Dax but her eyes were not really focused upon him. '*Mon dieu*,' he heard her mutter. 'So dark . . . *Non—je suis tromper, peut-être* . . .'

Principal Wood and Owen were staring at her, anxiously. The principal said, 'Paulina?' and took her hand, and at that point she flinched and snapped her eyes fully open. They were all silent for a few seconds. The *scent* that Dax had picked up seemed to pulse once and then fade. Paulina Sartre drew a long breath and turned to look at Principal Wood. He looked back, arching one eyebrow and waiting for her to speak.

'It's fine,' she said, at length.

'Have you found us another one?' asked Principal Wood.

'No,' she said. 'No . . . I think it was . . . it was something else.' She beamed suddenly, almost briskly. 'Nothing for you to worry about,' she said, and everybody relaxed slightly.

'I'm sorry if I scared you, Dax,' she said, now smiling warmly at him. 'I sometimes have portents—visions— little daydreams. They come at the most awkward times. And sometimes they mean not a fig. Enjoy your time here, Dax. You are very special.'

Owen rested his hand on Dax's shoulder and guided him back out of the office.

Dax was silent as they stepped outside. He saw Gideon waiting just beyond the conservatory area, on the edge of the quad.

'You OK, Dax? Did that spook you a bit?' said Owen.

'It was a bit weird,' confessed Dax. He didn't mention the smell. He didn't understand what had made Paulina Sartre feel that sudden dread, but he hoped it had nothing to do with *him*.

'Like she said, it can happen at any time. One of the downsides of the job.'

'What did she mean, before?' asked Dax. 'She kept going on about being worried about me and stuff. Why?'

Owen chuckled. 'Don't worry too much, Dax. She frets about every single student in the college. She's the one that finds you all, you see. When there's another COLA on the way, Mrs Sartre always knows a few days beforehand. She literally picked out your home on the map and sent me there. And she *saw* a few of the things that happened to you. She's a dowser and a seer and an empath.'

'What's a seer—and an empath?' asked Dax. He had a dim idea what a dowser was—one of those people who wave sticks and find water.

'Well, a seer literally *sees* stuff that most people can't. Sometimes before it happens, although Paulina Sartre tends mostly to see it *as* it's happening, anywhere in the country, in her mind. An empath has very strong intuition for what people are feeling and what makes them tick. So, with you, for instance, she picked up on your murderous feelings towards your delightful stepmother.'

Dax stopped dead by the aquarium and stared at Owen.

'It's all right,' said Owen. 'Frankly, if my stepmother locked me out of the house without food for several hours, I'd feel pretty murderous too. You're not too pleased with your dad, either—but that's another story. There's nothing *wrong* with the way you feel, Dax. You can't help it and, for my money, you've kept remarkable control of it all these years. But the problem with all that control is that it can eventually blow—right when you need it the most. That might be OK in an ordinary person, but it's pretty dangerous in a shapeshifter or a telekinetic or— heaven forbid—a pyrokinetic. You need to find ways of letting off that anger, bit by bit, so it's not quite such a powder keg. We'll help you do that here. Now—go off with Gideon. He'll look after you—in his own warped fashion—and give you a proper tour. Stick with him and have fun and I'll see you in class on Monday.'

Owen gave his shoulder a reassuring pat and strode off. Dax wandered over to Gideon, who was flipping a coin into the air and then bringing it down very slowly to his palm in steady, helter-skelter curves. Dax gazed at it in admiration.

'You all right then, Daxy-boy?' said Gideon, tucking the coin into his pocket. 'Seen Mrs Sartre and Mr Wood? Hang on . . . ' He pulled a square of something shiny from the same pocket and excavated two battered chunks of chocolate from their foil wrapping. He handed them to Dax. 'Go on. You'll feel better afterwards. It's always a bit weird when you first meet Mrs Sartre. Really freaked me out. I thought her eyes were going to go white and she was going to start spewing pea soup and spinning in the air or something.' Dax laughed and put one of the dubious chunks of chocolate in his mouth. It *was* comforting. 'Come on,' said Gideon, heading out of the quad, 'I'll show you around properly.'

He led Dax back up the stone steps and winding pathways past the small, rounded dwellings he'd seen last night. 'These are staff quarters,' he explained. 'Most of the teachers have got one of these. They look small, but they go right back into the cliff. Cute, aren't they? Cornish piskie houses!' He laughed and then dragged Dax on up the steps until they reached the door in the tall stone chimney where he'd first arrived.

'What *is* this place?' asked Dax, as they reached the doorway and the thick stone wall which lay between them and the terrifying drop to the sea and rocks below.

'It used to be an old tin mine,' said Gideon. 'Most of the workings and the boiler house are gone now, and this is what's left. Apparently, somewhere around here there's a shaft which drops down a hundred and fifty fathoms. Way below the sea level. Anyway, now this bit's the college gatehouse. There's no other way to get in or out, unless you're a very good rock climber or a seagull. Hey!' he paused and peered at Dax, speculatively. 'Do you shapeshift into a bird by any chance?'

Dax shook his head. 'No. A fox.'

Gideon considered this for a moment, pursing his lips. 'Could be useful,' he concluded and then knocked and pushed open the gatehouse door. Mr Pengalleon and Barber both looked up from the couch in the circular room. The gatekeeper was reading the papers and Barber had been resting his chin on his master's feet.

'Good morning, boys,' said Mr Pengalleon. 'Have you got a green slip?'

'Yes,' said Gideon and handed over the two bits of printed green paper. 'We have to get signed permission to go out,' he explained to Dax, as Mr Pengalleon got up and tapped a code number into the incongruous polished steel security plate on the frame of the thick oak front door. Dax glanced around the floor, wondering about the 150 fathom shaft. He saw no sign of a trapdoor. He tried to imagine what it would be like, falling 150 fathoms down a mine shaft, and hoped that the floor was as strong as it looked. Probably there was nothing but rock underneath anyway.

'Where are we going?' he asked, as they waved to Mr Pengalleon and Barber and walked across a patch of gravel towards the road. 'Aren't you supposed to be showing me around the college?'

'Yes. But I'm starting from the top. You'll get the best view of it from the wood. That's part of the college, too, but it's outside the perimeter, so we have to have permission. Come on, I'll show you.' He darted up a grassy bank towards a dark wood, which thickly covered the hill above them. Its trees were densely gathered at the top and then spread down across the lower slopes until they seemed to sprawl right over the cliff edge; tough knots of root and branch, clutching out into the high sea air.

Gideon led Dax to the foot of one of these trees and they settled into its strong network of roots, which formed a jutting seat on the edge of the rocky precipice. The cliff below fell away steeply, but it wasn't quite sheer. Further down Dax could see tufts of wiry grass and lichen and seabirds roosting on ledges. And the view—what a view! The college lay spread out below them like a village, its high glass windows sparkling in the sun. From chimneys in some of the small, round, cob houses nestling into the cliff, smoke was rising. Ant-like students were walking and running and idling in corners around the quad and on the sports field. Between the sports field promontory and the main college which neighboured it there was a small inlet, protected, a little way out to sea, by a circle of rocks which cradled the water and kept it smooth and glassy compared to the churning ink of the sea all around it. That must be the lido, thought Dax, and even now there were two brave souls jumping in, ignoring the October chill.

'This is the most amazing place I've ever been,' said Dax, then he nearly fell over the cliff with shock. An explosion had rocked the air and a large cloud of orange smoke was funnelling up near the fountain in the quad.

11

Dax scrambled to his feet and clung to one of the low branches near him, looking wildly around at Gideon. But the boy was still sitting down, casually levitating some twigs and leaves and making them perform a dance over the edge of the cliff. ''S all right,' he said, calmly, not taking his eyes off the little performance he was creating. 'It's just Spook. He's always at it.'

'What?' demanded Dax, sitting back down next to him. Gideon looked round and immediately the twigs and leaves dropped.

'Spook Williams. He's an illusionist—that's another kind of glamour. Sometimes he's pretty good, but most times he's a bit patchy. He wants to go into showbiz, so he's always messing around with pyrotechnics, getting used to walking out of a cloud of smoke.'

Dax was puzzled. 'But I thought illusionists, like you see on TV, I thought they did it all with mirrors and wires and stuff,' he said. 'I mean—it's not *real*, is it?'

'Of course it's not, dummy,' cackled Gideon. 'Why else would they be called illusionists? And they like it that way. They like people to think it's all about little gadgets and tricks and for some of them that's all it *is*. But the good ones . . . the *really* good ones—they actually do have powers, powers to hypnotize people into seeing something that isn't there or isn't happening. Trouble is, if people really cottoned on to this they'd be running out of theatres screaming. So the best illusionists are those who play it like a double agent. You never know when it's real illusion and you never know when it's fake illusion. Get it?'

'Sort of,' said Dax, rather confused. 'So, if this boy—Spook?—if he decided he wants us all to see a wall of giant squids or something, that's what we all see, is it? Even though it's not there?'

Gideon laughed again and got up, leading Dax back into the woods. 'He *wishes*. He's not that good. It's just little bits of glamour from time to time. He convinced me that my lunch was full of snails once. Git.' They walked on, treading carefully around the roots of old trees which rose like tense knuckles out of the soft peat and needles around them. It was quiet in the wood and smelt of dying leaves and newborn mushrooms. Dax felt utterly comfortable there, although he was often distracted by tiny movements and had to fight the urge to stop and forage after whatever was making them. 'No,' he told himself, quietly. 'No more spiders. Ever.'

'What's that?' said Gideon, and to his surprise, Dax found himself telling his new friend all about the day he'd first turned into a fox. Gideon was riveted and shouted out in delighted disgust when he heard about the spider-eating incident. He clapped Dax on the shoulder and said, 'Mate! We are going to have *such* a good time. Can you do it now? Can you change here? Nobody would see except me.'

Dax shook his head regretfully. 'No. I've tried it a few times and sometimes I *think* it's going to happen, but then it doesn't. Owen—Mr Hind—reckons that I can learn how, though. Wow—that's spooky!'

They had come to the perimeter of the little wood and below them the ground sloped away slightly and dipped into a wide, shallow basin of marshland, bordered to their left by a drop to the sea and far away to their right by a gentle rise which would eventually meet the coastal road, Dax guessed. A path wound through the marsh, looking well gravelled and fairly dry, and there was a wooden bridge in the distance, spanning what looked like lush green grass. The marsh was dotted with thousands of shaggy tussocks of bog weed which rose as high as a man's chest. The lower-lying areas were shrouded in a thin, opaque mist. To Dax it smelt peaty and rich and dangerous.

'It's OK to cross, as long as you stick to the path,' said Gideon. 'But you don't want to mess around. They reckon this marsh has swallowed a cow whole. That bit, where the bridge is, goes down for *ever*, under that green stuff. There are signs up warning walkers not to let their dogs off the leash—or else,' he dropped his voice dramatically.

They returned to the wood and made their way back to the college grounds. Gideon showed him the library, the gym hall, and finally the small post room. 'We all get a pigeonhole,' he said, showing Dax a long wooden unit full of tiny drawers, each with a small nameplate. Dax was pleased to find a drawer with his own name there. 'You collect your post and your allowance money here. Allowance day is Monday,' went on Gideon.

Dax shrugged. 'Doesn't matter what day it is. There's no way Gina will send *me* any money.'

'No?' Gideon pulled a sympathetic face. 'Ah well, don't worry. You'll still get COLA money.'

'COLA money?'

'Yep. Everyone here gets a small allowance each week. Because there are some kids, like you, whose families haven't got much. It's not a lot but it's better than nothing.'

'Oh, how touching. Another charity case.' Dax spun round to see a tall boy with ginger hair leaning against the post room wall with his arms folded, eyeing Dax with amusement. 'You must be Dax Jones,' he said and held out a slightly droopy hand. Dax wasn't keen, but he went to shake it anyway. As he did so, the hand was swiftly withdrawn and with a small buzz and a pop there was a shower of glitter in the air, which blew right into his face, stinging his eyes and sharply tickling his nose.

Dax coughed and shouted, 'Hey!'

Gideon, also spluttering, said, 'Cut it out, Spook!'

'Dax Jones,' said the boy, again, walking languidly round him and looking him up and down. 'So *you're* what everyone's so excited about. Our very first shapeshifter.' Abruptly he leaned in, putting his mouth right up to

Dax's ear, and said in a low voice, 'They usually end up dead before they get here. Be careful, skin-walker.'

Dax shoved him violently away as a sudden burst of anger shot up through him. Adroitly, he then pushed it down before it could get the better of him, but his voice still shook slightly when he said, 'I am *not* a skin-walker.'

'Oh,' said Spook, lightly, as if he'd just put sugar in someone's tea by mistake. 'I'm sorry. I didn't mean to offend you. If you prefer "shapeshifter" that's absolutely fine. Bye, Gideon. Got that football three feet up yet?' And he was gone.

'Git,' said Gideon, again. 'Don't waste your breath. He's just jealous.'

'Why?' asked Dax, flicking little bits of glitter off his sleeves. 'What's his problem?'

'I think he wishes he was a tele,' said Gideon, loftily. 'Well, I mean—what use is an illusionist? You can only make people see stuff that's not there. But *teles*—well, we can actually *do* stuff. Really make things happen. And *you* actually *do* change. It's not just a mind trick, is it?'

'No,' said Dax, thinking of how very *real* being a fox felt.

'*And* he thinks he's better than us,' went on Gideon as they wandered back out into the quad. Spook could be seen holding court with three other boys, sitting on the edge of the fountain pool. 'His parents are really loaded. Big country estate in Devon. When he found out me and my dad live in a council house he wouldn't even sit next to me in class.' The boys with Spook suddenly turned and looked towards them. Spook leaned in and said something in a low voice and they all laughed.

Gideon strode off. 'Come on, Dax, don't give 'em the satisfaction.'

By the end of the day, Dax had the college mapped out pretty well in his mind. Gideon told him that the local village was about half an hour's walk from the gate tower and that you could get permission to go out in pairs at weekends, between set hours. 'We'll go out next weekend if you like,' he said. 'There's a really good chocolate parlour down there. And an excellent fresh fish-and-chip cafe. But I've got a match tomorrow—I'm a striker in the Tregarren Tigers, didn't you know?' he said proudly. 'You want to watch? You any good at football?'

'I'm not bad,' said Dax. 'I'll come and watch.'

The next day was cooler, with a pale grey, low sky. Dax wore his coat and scarf to cheer Gideon on from the sidelines. About twenty other students were scattered along the edge of the pitch, too, and Barry came to keep him company. 'You don't play too, then?' asked Dax.

'Nah,' said Barry. 'They don't trust me.' He seemed quite philosophical about this.

'Why not?' asked Dax. Barry seemed like an honest kind of boy.

Barry shrugged and looked a bit sheepish. 'I can't help it, but I just *fade out* a bit when I'm doing a tackle.'

'Fade out?' echoed Dax.

'You know—do the disappearing thing,' said Barry. 'I'm not even that good at it, but when everyone's running

109

around and we're about to score and then I'm . . . well, you know, *not there*—even just a bit *thin*, well, they reckon I'm cheating.'

Dax stared at Barry, fascinated. 'Go on!' he urged. 'Do it! Disappear!' But Barry shifted self-consciously in his thick anorak, and wouldn't. Dax turned back to the game between the Tigers and the Terrors, as the two sides called themselves. It was definitely going the Tigers' way, he was pleased to see, and even now Gideon was tearing down the pitch, controlling the ball and aiming for the goal. There were boys *and* girls playing, Dax noticed. He recognized one or two faces from around the college, including Spook Williams who was lankily running down one side of the pitch in a Terrors' strip. Dax watched as the boy caught up with a team-mate and whispered something to him. The other boy grinned and did a thumbs-up sign, keeping his eyes on Gideon who was preparing to shoot at goal. And then Spook slowed to a halt, let his hands swing down to his sides, and *stared* at the goal end. He smiled and tilted his chin down, peering harder than ever from under his brows, across the pitch. In the path of his gaze the ground seemed to shudder very slightly, as if in a heat haze in the middle of summer.

When Gideon shot it went embarrassingly wide, but instead of groaning and slumping, the Tigers team, to a player, stopped in their tracks, confused, and then all swiftly turned round and began shouting and complaining at the referee. 'What happened?' asked Dax, bewildered.

Barry was huffing and making that whistling noise through his nose. 'Spook Williams, I'll bet!' he snorted, heatedly. 'That's just his style. Watch! Yep—he's getting a card.'

The referee, a gym teacher who also coached both teams, strode across to Spook, who was pulling a hurt 'What did *I* do?' kind of face, and gave him a warning before striding away. Spook appeared to protest, but the ref turned and gave him a very hard stare and the boy held up his hands and could be heard murmuring, 'OK, OK! It was just a joke!'

'What happened?' asked Dax, again.

'Didn't you see it?' asked Barry, looking at him curiously.

'See *what*?' Dax was getting exasperated.

'Spook shifted the goalposts,' said Barry. 'No, really—he did. He made it look like the goal was off to the left, so when Gideon shot he went wide. It was an illusion. It's the second time he's done that this term. I reckon they should kick him out of the team. They get puffed up enough about *me* fading out! But—are you sure you didn't see it?'

'No,' said Dax. 'I saw the ground go a bit wavy, but nothing else changed.'

Barry turned his face so that half of it disappeared into the hood of his anorak and one eye stared hard round the orange piping at Dax. 'Blimey,' was all he said, and his nose let out a long whistle.

* * *

'Blimey!' said Gideon, an hour later, back at the dorm. His nose didn't whistle, but his mouth did. He looked quickly at Barry and said, 'Does anyone else know?' Barry shook his head and both boys looked at Dax in grave fascination.

'*What?*' said Dax.

Gideon sat down, his hair still damp from the post-match shower. 'Dax—when the goalposts shifted, were you actually looking in that direction? Or were you looking at something else?'

'I was watching you—waiting for you to score. And then you muffed it.'

Gideon gave a sudden chuckle and clapped his hands with glee. 'He didn't see it! Spook didn't get it past him!' he laughed, excitedly. 'Don't you see what this means, Dax?' Dax shook his head. 'You're resistant to glamour! You don't get hooked into group illusions! That's *brilliant*! I don't think there's anyone else here that's a resistant! Maybe it's a shapeshifter thing; maybe it's because you've got fox vision or something. But it's fantastic!'

Dax grinned. 'So, you mean I can't be fooled with stuff that Spook does?'

'Or anyone else like him!' said Gideon. 'I mean— some of the stronger ones *might* get to you, but if you've got resistance now, to small fry like Spook, you might be able to build it up and resist *any* illusionist. You might even be able to see Barry! Barry—do it! Do it now, so we can check!' But Barry was still reluctant.

'There's too many people about,' he said, aware of

the noise of other boys trooping through the corridor outside. 'I might get seen . . . being *not* seen . . . '

'Oh, well, anyway,' Gideon turned back to Dax. 'Don't say anything to *anyone* about this. Promise me!'

'Not even Ow—Mr Hind?' said Dax, uneasily.

'Well, maybe him, if you must . . . '

'Maybe he *should* tell Principal Wood,' said Barry, gravely. 'You know . . . he's always saying his door's always open and all that.'

'No,' said Dax, so quickly and resolutely that the other two looked at him in surprise. 'No—I . . . I think you're right about keeping this to ourselves,' went on Dax, hastily. He couldn't explain why, but he really didn't want the principal to know. 'I won't tell anyone else, unless it's really important. You'll just have to help me to play along when anyone does something I can't see.'

'You're going to be really handy to have around,' beamed Gideon. 'Dax versus Spook! One–Nil!'

Lessons resumed on Monday morning and for Dax it was maddening. Here he was, sharing a college with the most extraordinary children in the world, and they all had to sit at desks doing geography or maths or English! Gideon had told him that special powers were *not* to be exercised during class. Of course, people *did* sometimes give in to temptation, but they were likely to end up with half an allowance or on dishwashing duty in the canteen if they were caught.

The teachers seemed so normal that Dax did wonder,

briefly, if they actually *knew* about the stuff their students could do. In the afternoon Mrs Dann, a slight, dark-haired woman in a thick green cardigan, was writing up a list of Scandinavian countries with her back to the class. Dax was beginning to feel sleepy and then he heard the faintest of smothered giggles and a whistling noise behind him and saw that Barry's pencil was flicking abstractedly in the air—and nobody was there to flick it. At first he thought it was Gideon, but the boy was right next to him, dozing with his chin resting on his palm. Dax peered around again and saw that there was a rubber band about to be pinged in the direction of the waggling pencil. Whoever was about to ping was also invisible.

Dax glanced back towards Mrs Dann, anxiously. He was just about to nudge Gideon awake when the teacher paused at the whiteboard. In a sudden, fluid movement, she put the marker she'd been using on the shelf beneath it and picked up a small silver can. And then she spun round, bellowing, 'Barry Blake and Jennifer Troke! Don't you move!' and expelled a hard jet of green spray across the two empty desks. At once a bizarre image of Barry and Jennifer appeared, picked out in green edges. There was enough spray on their faces for the class to make out how worried and guilty they looked, even semi-transparent.

Mrs Dann sighed, put down the can, and rested her hands on her hips. 'Barry, if you want your invisibility to be effective, you really should get your adenoids done. You sound like a possessed tin whistle. And Jennifer, you should know better than to get caught up in a prank like this.'

'But she dared *me*!' howled Barry, who was now appearing again, pink and embarrassed beneath the green spray. Jennifer, too, was becoming more substantial by the second; she was anxiously rubbing the green coating off her spectacles.

'Enough!' said Mrs Dann. 'Both of you—down to the principal's office to ask him to cancel next week's allowance. And then get cleaned up and go straight on to your next class.'

Barry and Jennifer slunk out of the classroom and Mrs Dann surveyed the remainder of her students with a raised eyebrow. 'If any of the rest of you are tempted to try out a little nonsense, please remember that I have a whole armoury of anti-glamour within reach.' Nobody spoke and several of them sat up straight. 'Well, then,' said Mrs Dann, crisply. 'Back to Scandinavia.'

12

After geography, Dax checked his timetable again and asked Gideon where they went to get to Development class, whatever that was.

'We don't. *You* do,' said Gideon, rifling through his bag for a little post-lesson chocolate. 'It'll be a one-to-one session for you, with Mr Hind or Mr Eades, or maybe Mrs Sartre.'

'What—just me?' asked Dax.

'Yep. Well, you're the only shapeshifter here, so it can't be in a group. We all get Development on our own sometimes, usually when we first arrive, but then we get into groups and work together. I'll go in with all the other telekinetics and Barry will go in with a group of other vanishers and then Spook'll go in with a bunch of *talentless conjurors*.'

He said this loud enough for Spook to hear, as the boy passed them in the corridor. Spook smirked over his shoulder and said, 'Eat snails, Reader.'

Gideon went on, guiding Dax down the corridor. 'You'll get all the healers and all the mediums in their own groups too. Then the psychics, and the clairvoyants, clairaudients, and so on.'

'Blimey,' murmured Dax. 'It must be amazing in those sessions.'

'It's damn *loud*, that's for sure,' said Gideon. 'All those spirits trying to get a word in edgeways: trances, possessions, knocking . . . it's a scrum. Still, they can be quite useful. We *never* plan a big match only to get rained off. And sometimes you get one of these.'

He pulled a crumpled pink slip of paper from his pocket and handed it to Dax. The paper was a small printed form with **SPIRIT COMMUNICATION NOTICE** at the top. Underneath it read:

TO: *(and **Gideon Reader** was written in pencil)*
FROM: *Jessica Moorland*
The above medium/clairvoyant/audient has been contacted by spirit NAMED: *Auntie Pam* **who wish/es you to know that:** *You are doing really well and will soon find your string.*
THIS COMMUNICATION IS AUTHORIZED BY: *Mr Eades*

The name at the end was a signature. Dax gazed up at Gideon in awe. 'You mean this message really came from your dead auntie?'

'Yep,' said Gideon. 'It's the third one I've had from Auntie Pam this term.'

'And what about your string? Have you found it? It must mean something important.'

'Nah,' said Gideon, pushing open a door to a narrow stairwell that Dax hadn't been into before. 'I don't know *what* she's on about. Dozy rabbit never makes any sense. But it's nice that she keeps in touch.'

He left Dax to go down the stairs. 'Through the doors and to the right—B12 is yours, I expect. Seeya.'

The long basement corridor was lit with pale globes, carpeted, and painted light green. Dax noted the numbers on the doors that appeared regularly down either side and saw B12 at the far end to his right. He knocked on the door and went in to what looked a bit like a dance studio. One entire wall was taken up with a mirror and the other three were bare brick, painted the same soft green as outside. The floor was carpeted in green and wall lights sent a soft glow out from each corner. The room was empty except for one small bookcase near the door, filled with reference books and a sizeable first-aid kit attached to the wall above it, and two chairs and one small table arranged along a wall. A second door led off into the opposite corner. It was incredibly quiet.

Dax padded across to the mirror and regarded himself in it. He looked different. As if he'd been 'switched on'. There was a healthy colour in his skin; he didn't look so pale under his thick dark hair. His brown eyes looked bright. He guessed it was the excellent food and sea air.

He jumped as the door swung open and in came Owen with another man who was carrying a clipboard and some papers. The man was wearing a grey suit and had a tired face and wispy grey hair. He looked at Dax over the top of his horn-rimmed spectacles and raised his eyebrows.

'This is the boy?' he said to Owen, as if Dax was a specimen.

'Yes—Dax—this is Mr Eades,' said Owen, striding over to him. 'He'll be sitting in on our sessions.'

'Just pretend I'm not here,' said Mr Eades, gravely, in a voice like dried leaves in a breeze. He sat at the small table, depositing a sheaf of notepaper, a pen, and a small blue flask upon it.

'OK,' said Dax. He felt oddly nervous. Mr Eades gave him a curt nod and turned his attention to his notes.

'Can you make him do it?' he said to Owen, again, as if Dax wasn't in the room.

'Not so far, not without Triple Eight,' replied Owen. 'But we haven't really got started yet. OK! Dax, let's start with some breathing exercises.'

Perplexed, Dax did as he was told. He lay down on the soft carpet and closed his eyes and began to breathe more deeply, as instructed. Owen told him to concentrate on scrunching up first his feet and then letting them relax, then up to his calves, and then relaxing, and then up to his knees and so on, until he got right up to his scalp. By this time, Dax *was* feeling remarkably relaxed.

Owen was sitting a little way off, cross-legged on the floor. He had dimmed the lights and now he spoke in a very calm, slow voice. 'Dax, I want you to picture a place where you've been which made you feel safe,' he said. Dax thought of the wood above the college. 'I want you to imagine you are there now and that you're lying down, very comfortably, as you are now. I'm going to count to five, and as I count, I want you to sink deeper into sleep, wrapped up in the safety and peace of the place you are in.'

As Owen counted steadily from one to five, Dax felt as if he were slowly drifting down. For a while Owen said nothing and Dax was content to drift. He could feel the peaty earth soft under his shoulder blades and smell the fungi and disintegrating leaves. The birds were cheeping a gentle chorus in the trees above him and a warm sun dappled down through the branches and touched his skin. His breathing was deep and regular and even though he *knew* he was still in B12 and could hear every noise there, the wood felt more real to him.

'Now, Dax,' went on Owen, softly. 'I want you to remember the first time you turned into a fox. I want you to think back to where you were and what was happening, just before you changed.'

Still feeling safe in the wood, Dax found a picture of the interior of the shed back at home opening up in his mind. He looked around it dispassionately and noticed the dust and cobwebs, the bags of peat, and the balls of raffia. He began to smell it. A small tremor ran up through him and he shivered.

'OK, Dax. I need you to remember *exactly* how you were feeling,' said Owen, somewhere off to his right. Behind Owen, Mr Eades rustled a paper. And someone else moved, too. Dax pulled his mind back into the shed and its heat and its *smell*.

Dax didn't want to feel it, but he didn't seem to

be able to stop the sudden punch of panic that hit him, along with a thick inhalation of white spirit and suffocating heat. He was aware of his breathing speeding up, speeding up, speeding up . . . There was a sudden crack across his mind and he felt a belt of power, like an electric shock, crashing through him and he cried out— *actually* cried out in B12. Now he was dragging hot air into his lungs with a terrible rasping noise and coughing and shouting. Suddenly he was aware of somebody holding his shoulders.

'Dax! Dax!' Owen was shouting. 'I'm bringing you back. Hear me! Hear me! Listen, I'm counting you back in—5-4-3-2-1. Dax! Wake up!'

Dax opened his eyes and stared, dazed, at Owen, who was still gripping his shoulders and looking very concerned. Sitting up, Dax realized his chin was wet and wiped it quickly, embarrassed.

Owen released his grip and sat back on his heels, looking concerned. 'You,' he said, 'are not going to be easy.'

Mr Eades had put down his notes and now he came across with a cup of lemonade, which he had apparently supplied from his flask. 'You need sugar,' explained Owen, and Dax, his hands still shaking, gladly accepted the cup. 'We'll try again another day,' added Owen.

'Do we have to?' Dax wasn't keen. He liked the lying around in woods bit very much, but wished he could just stay there. He glanced around the room as he sipped the sweet bubbles. He had felt sure someone else had come in while he had been under hypnosis, but nobody else was there.

'I'm trying to find a trigger for you,' said Owen. 'We need something to work with, to get you to the stage when you can bring on a transformation at will. And then, ideally, to stop it again without the need to fall asleep. But it's very early days. You took to the hypnotherapy really well. It's just that, even while you're under, you're exerting a bit too much control. If you weren't so good at keeping everything in check and fighting off your emotions, you would probably have just retraced the path of what happened to you the first time you changed, and very likely you would have changed again.'

Dax didn't know what to say. He drank his lemonade and noticed that Mr Eades was back at his seat, scribbling notes. After a few minutes, when he was feeling steadier, Owen said he could finish school for the day. 'We usually put these sessions in the late afternoon, because they can be exhausting and there's no point trying to go off and do maths afterwards,' he explained. 'Go and get some sea air. I'll see you in class tomorrow.'

'Oh—what do you teach?' asked Dax, trying to remember his timetable. Owen would probably be doing physics or chemistry, he guessed.

'Woodwork,' said Owen.

'Woodwork?'

'That's me. I have a way with dovetail joints.'

Surprised, and still slightly dazed, Dax left B12. Outside the sea air immediately began to revive him.

The campus was quiet: there were still twenty minutes or so until the end of classes for the day. Dax wandered around the winding paths until he found himself on the edge of the sports field and leaning over its sturdy fence to gaze at the crashing waves below. He could feel the spray in his face, although the foaming water was a good seven metres beneath him, curling desperately around some glistening rocks and then being dragged back to the ocean, in endless repetition.

At first he thought the *other* noise he could hear was a desolate seabird, crying for its mate. Then he realized that it was a person. A girl. Dax leaned further over the fence, scanning the grassy ledge that fell away steeply on the other side. Then he saw a pair of neat, glittery, purple trainers with matching socks. The feet and legs that went into them were poking out of what was evidently a small cave in the rock. Dax scrambled up over the fence and dropped, carefully, to the other side. The narrow strip of grass gave way to lichen and wiry weed, clinging to the rocky edge before it dropped away to the sea. Dax edged along it towards the trainers and the sound of crying and, kneeling down, swung his head down beneath the ledge to see who they belonged to.

Sitting, hugging her knees in misery, was Lisa Hardman. Her back was up against the wall of the shallow cave she had found and her neat new jeans and thick fleece were mucked up with grass and earth stains. Clearly she had wanted to get into her hiding place pretty badly. Dax had never seen her yet with a hair out of place.

Realizing she was being watched, Lisa glared up at him. 'What are you doing? Spying on me? Go away!'

Dax slid down to the cave and knelt to talk to her. 'I'm not spying. I've just been let out of Development and I needed some sea air. I didn't know you were here.'

'Well, now you do. So leave me alone,' she said. Her dark blue eyes were puffy and wet and she was now scrubbing at them fiercely with a screwed-up tissue.

'What are you so upset about? Don't you like it here?' persisted Dax.

'I don't care where I am,' she said bitterly. 'It doesn't make any difference.'

'*What* doesn't make any difference?' asked Dax, ignoring the fierce look on her face.

'Nothing! Nowhere! It doesn't stop, no matter where I am. Not even when I'm asleep. It doesn't stop.'

Dax tried to sit next to her but she wouldn't make any space for him, so he continued crouching on the ledge, anchoring his fingers in some tough, knotted weed in the rock, to be sure he didn't slip. 'What's your thing, then? What do you do?'

'Oh, why won't you go *away*?' she wailed, but she seemed about to say more, so Dax stayed put. 'I—I see things. And hear things. And feel things.' Her lower lip shook and she pressed her fingers to it for a moment, making it stop. 'I find lost things, and lost . . . ' she gulped mournfully, ' . . . lost *people*. And I get *warnings* and messages and stuff. And none of it, Dax Jones, *none* of it is nice. And I don't want it, but it won't stop. So that's it.

124

Don't expect me to go all sweet and trancey just for *you* because I don't do it. I'm not playing along. I didn't ask for this and I'm not going to help.' She folded her arms and stared angrily out to sea.

Dax felt some sympathy for her. It sounded pretty hard. 'But doesn't it help to be here?' he asked, tentatively. 'Can't they help you, in Development?'

'Nobody can help me,' she said bleakly. 'And I'm not helping *them*. I didn't ask for this stupid thing and I didn't ask to come here. So, sorry. Thank you for being nice, but sorry. It's not going to happen.'

Dax nodded and began to climb back up the path. He was surprised when he heard her call. 'Dax . . . ?'

'Yes?' he shouted back.

'*Only* because you're letting me alone, I'll just say this . . . When you get back over the fence, drop to your knees.'

Dax shook his head. The girl was probably barmy. But as he scrambled back over the fence, he did, indeed, drop to his knees, and in the second that he did there was a vicious thud inches above his head and a hard-kicked football whacked into the panel.

He scooped up the ball and threw it back down to some boys on the pitch. 'Thanks, Lisa,' he called back over the fence. She didn't reply.

13

Dax enjoyed Owen's woodwork class. It was only sparsely attended. Apparently, you could opt out of it and do pottery instead, if you liked, and only about twelve students had chosen to stick with woodwork. This suited Dax fine. He was surprised to see that both Mia and Lisa were in the class. Barry wasn't, but Gideon was, and the two boys teamed up to make a box, using proper dovetailing and no glue. Owen was very keen on using only natural substances to create things and the shelves were full of boxes and baskets and tools created with wood, twigs, fine strips of bark, and dried, twisted root woven into reliable knots and stitching.

Dax loved the smell of wood shavings and sap and the feel of rough grain under his fingers. He found he was quite good at cutting the precise notches they needed to fit the pieces of box together.

The class was quiet and focused and for the moment, completely normal. Dax found it was relaxing to be in such a class. Owen would wander among them, offering advice and occasionally demonstrating a technique for sawing or chiselling, and two hours passed gently as the students were absorbed in their efforts. As they packed up their tools at the end of the afternoon, Owen said,

'I'm starting up some woodsman classes next week. I can show you how to make things outdoors—we get to go up to the woods above the college. Anyone who wants to join me can put their names on the list by the door.'

Dax made a bee-line for the list and was surprised to see Lisa already there, marking her name firmly on the paper. She glanced at him with less hostility than usual, and walked out of the class. Dax added his name and so did Mia and Gideon. Nobody else did. Dax guessed they weren't so keen on being outdoors as the Cornish autumn edged into winter. He was pleased that Mia would be coming, because he still found her presence wonderfully calming. He had, as Gideon had predicted, become a little less entranced. His 'immunity' had built up a little during that morning in class with Mia. For the first two hours he had been barely able to tear his eyes away from the back of her head.

Mrs Dann had noticed his state and not said anything. She was well aware that pupils had to get used to Mia before they could concentrate. Fortunately, by lunchtime, Dax could read a whole page of *Twentieth Century World History* without looking up, and then the woodwork had absorbed him so much that he only got the odd wave of warmth when Mia passed by. He was getting hold of himself.

Before tea, he and Gideon checked in at the post room and Dax found a small white envelope with a £5 note in it. 'It's your COLA allowance,' said Gideon. 'It's a bit late, because you've only just got here.' He also found a letter, redirected from the post office in the village (no mail arrived directly at Tregarren College), with writing that he recognized. Clive's neat, backwards-slanting script was inked across it, with the Bark's End postmark. Dax tore it open, feeling as if he hadn't seen Clive for a year, rather than just a few days. He remembered he'd asked Gina to phone through the college post office box address to Clive and was surprised to see that she must have done it.

'*Dear Dax,*' Clive had written,

'*I hope you're happy at your new school. It's not the same here without you—but I don't think it would be the same anyway. Matthew still hasn't come back to school and Toby is so quiet and nervous in class that none of us really know what to do around him. Sometimes he even sucks his thumb. I've been all geared up to say that I conjured up a skin-walker and frighten the pants off the pair of them, but I haven't really needed that. Dax, your work here is done!*

'*Anyway, the main point of this letter is to warn you. We had that reporter come round to the house, asking questions. Apparently she's been to see Matthew's family and found out more about what happened on that day. I didn't say anything to her, of course, and my mum told her to go away or she'd call the police. Anyway, the reporter went off, but she was really suspicious, and she sat outside, watching the house from her car for a while, talking on her mobile phone.*

'*Anyway, I've put the cutting in, so you know what to expect. I doubt she'll be able to find you where you are now, but just so you know.*

Regards from Clive
PS. I made another paper clock and got ten house points.'

Dax grinned and then dug his fingers back into the envelope and found a cut out piece of newspaper. He unfolded it with curiosity and some anxiety.

WILD ANIMAL ATTACK ON PUPILS screamed the headline. It went on: **Two Bark's End schoolboys received treatment for bites and scratches following a mysterious attack in the basement at their school.**

Matthew Spacey, 12, and Toby Rogers, 11, were in the caretaker's storeroom with two other pupils when, they claim, they were viciously attacked by some kind of wild dog. Parents of other pupils at the school say their children were shocked to see the two boys running, screaming and bleeding, down the corridors.

'We don't know what it was, but it makes you quite worried, that a school could allow a wild, vicious animal in,' said one mother, Christine Broderick, from Anglesea Court, Bark's End. (Well, they let Matthew and Toby in, thought Dax, with a snort.)

'We've all been a bit scared by it, but the school say the whole building was searched and they didn't find any animal at all.'

Head teacher Geoffrey Clegg issued a statement to parents in a handout. He said: 'We are concerned that two of our pupils were apparently in some kind of scuffle with a dog, in the basement. Pupils are

not allowed in the basement, but nevertheless, we take our children's safety very seriously and have conducted a thorough search of the premises. We have found nothing to suggest there is any danger to pupils and are taking all measures to ensure that no animals are able to gain access to the school and its grounds.'

But the school refused to comment on why the other two boys, allegedly in the basement with Matthew and Toby, have not been officially named, or why one of them was apparently moved to a new school the following day.

The injured boys' parents declined to comment, and the parents of a third boy, who may have witnessed the incident, refused to speak about the case.

If you know anything about the BEAST OF BARK'S END, please contact the newsdesk . . .

Dax hooted with laughter. The Beast of Bark's End! Gideon looked up from unwrapping the parcel of chocolate his dad had sent him. Dax handed him the cutting and Gideon gaped and grinned as he read through it.

'The Beast of Bark's End,' he said, admiringly. 'That's brilliant! I'm sharing a dorm with a legend!'

Dax took the cutting to Owen Hind, knocking on the door of one of the little round cob cottages that Gideon had pointed out to him. A ribbon of smoke was curling out of the stubby chimney up on the conical roof, and it smelt of wood and berries. Owen opened the door and Dax stood awkwardly on the step for a moment, before handing him the cutting and Clive's letter. His concern for Clive hadn't quite gone.

Owen glanced quickly at the cutting, caught the headline, and then pulled Dax into the cottage and shut the door behind him. His reaction was less buoyant than Gideon's. He read the report quickly, without a word, and then sighed heavily, rubbing his chin and furrowing his brow. 'Sit down,' he said to Dax, sinking into a worn leather chair by the small brick fireplace, and turning his attention to Clive's letter.

Dax sat in a wooden rocking chair on the other side of the fire and looked around him. The room had a low ceiling with dark beams and the floor was tiled with stone, covered near the glowing fireplace with a large, dark red rug. Above the crackling log fire, on a narrow brick mantel, was a bronze Tilley storm-lantern, although the room, in the early winter twilight, was lit by an electric lamp on a stand behind Owen's chair. Piles of books and more wooden boxes and baskets lay around the curved edges of the uneven room and a rough brick arch led further back into what Dax presumed was Owen's kitchen and bathroom and sleeping quarters, deep inside the cliff.

'Who have you told about this?' said Owen, folding Clive's letter and sliding it back into the envelope with the cutting.

'Only Gideon,' said Dax. 'He loves being in a dorm with the Beast of Bark's End.'

Owen rolled his eyes as he handed the envelope back to Dax. 'Only Gideon. Oh dear.'

'She won't be able to find me here, will she?' asked Dax.

'It's unlikely, but I don't like the feel of this,' said Owen, thoughtfully. 'She's playing it by the book at the moment, being quite discreet—probably had a reporting restriction bounced on her because you're under sixteen. But when the press think up daft names, like the Loch Ness Monster or the Beast of Bodmin . . . or Bark's End, they tend to want to keep it all rolling for a while, to wring as much out of the story as they can. I think she'll be doing some digging. But no—I don't think she'll work out where you are. In the meantime, though, write back to your friend and ask him to send anything else that crops up in the paper—and keep me informed.'

But it seemed that there was nothing to worry about, because with his next letter, three days later, Clive said he hadn't read any more about the Beast of Bark's End.

'There's still talk about it, obviously,' he wrote. *'But Matthew's back at school now, although he won't sit anywhere near me* or *Toby. Both of them are still very quiet. It's heaven.'*

Dax hoped that was that. He was getting into the flow of things now, at COLA Club, and he and Gideon were becoming inseparable. Little by little he was getting an idea of what some of the children around him could do. In the evening and at the weekends the students gathered either in their dorm common room or joint common room, which lay between the boys' and the girls' dormitory buildings. In the larger joint common room they could watch TV at the television end or play assorted games at the other, study in a quiet area, or just lounge on the squashy blue sofas and talk. There were no computers or hi-tech games, Dax noticed.

'Not much point,' said Gideon. 'There's so much supernatural whatnot bouncing off the walls around here that the damn things were always freezing and crashing. The telly's always grainy too, but they left that. They took the computers away after I first got here, about four months ago. *And* I reckon,' he leaned conspiratorially towards Dax, 'they want to keep us cut off from the rest of the world!'

Dax looked at him sceptically. 'It's true,' protested Gideon. 'There's no way they're going to let us loose on the Internet, is there?'

'Who needs it?' said Jessica Moorland, passing the back of their sofa. 'Some of us have a perfectly good web of communication *without* an electric socket and a phone line. Your Auntie Pam says stop slouching.'

Gideon sat up straight and then narrowed his eyes suspiciously at Jessica. 'Sometimes I think that girl's winding me up,' he muttered at the back of her curly brown head as she walked on.

'And your birthmark *doesn't* look like a map of England—it's more of a triangle, she says,' called back Jessica. Gideon blushed.

'Where's your birthmark then?' asked Dax, laughing. 'Can I see?'

'No, you cannot,' said Gideon.

Although they were not supposed to use their powers outside Development, invariably, during their own time the students' supernatural abilities spilled over. Nobody seemed to be remotely surprised when three twelve-year-old girls began levitating fifty centimetres off the floor in the TV room, but they got asked to leave because their effort was interfering with the picture.

Barry would occasionally 'fade out', often in the company of Jennifer Troke, the willowy blonde girl with glasses who looked as if butter wouldn't melt in her mouth, but who'd got Barry into trouble in class. The trouble with Barry, apart from the adenoidal whistle that he gave when he breathed out, was that he wasn't great at keeping his presence a secret even when he remembered to breathe through his mouth. Sadly, he was naturally clumsy and would invariably stagger over a table or bash into someone and then flash back into sight looking deeply embarrassed. Jennifer carried it all off much better and was given to suddenly appearing at your elbow when you were reading, and remarking on your book. It was discomfiting, to say the least.

The mediums tended to stick together in groups, and you could never be sure, when they were talking, if they were addressing another student or someone from beyond the grave—or 'passed over', as Jessica said.

Mia often spent time with them, but this evening she

seemed happy to loll on the sofa by the fire with Dax, Gideon, and Barry. Dax made sure he took the opposite end; he didn't want the others to start giggling if he began staring again, even though he was fairly sure he was over the worst now. Gideon was working hard on lifting a book off her head smoothly and Mia was trying not to giggle. The leather-bound volume eased up nicely a few inches and then began to wobble, before toppling down on her shoulder. 'Ow!' she winced.

'Can you take away your own pain?' asked Dax, curiously, as Mia rubbed her shoulder briskly and Gideon looked very embarrassed.

'No, of course not,' laughed Mia. 'It doesn't work like that—but we can make ourselves feel better with our state of mind, if we work at it.'

Dax hugged his knees and stared into the red coals and blackening logs in the grate. 'What do you think this is all about? Us all coming here? Why us?'

'Search me,' shrugged Gideon. 'It doesn't make any sense at all. Maybe we're the terrifying result of some kind of lab experiment they did on our parents.' He nudged Barry into sight on the back of the sofa; the boy was working at his stuffed up nose with a ragged looking tissue. 'I mean— Barry *looks* like a terrifying lab experiment, doesn't he?'

'Oi, you—cut it out,' sniffed Barry and vanished again. They knew he was still there, though, by the whistling and snuffling.

'Do you think they'd try to stop anyone if they left?' mused Dax.

'Why—you planning to?' asked Gideon.

'Not on your life. I love it here!'

Gideon stretched back on the sofa and considered. 'I reckon they're probably just as confused as we are, the people that set this place up. They're probably a bit scared too—but they've got us sussed anyway, so we might as well wait and see what happens. And anyway, I live by the Mia Rule.'

Dax blinked. 'The Mia Rule?'

'Yep. Mia and all her mates are super-sensitive, right? If anything really sinister was going on, I reckon they'd pick it up. Right, Mia?'

Mia smiled her gentle smile and nodded. 'Yes. I think we would. And I think the clairvoyants would get warning too. And so far nothing seems too far amiss. I think we are meant to be together and there's a reason for all this. I just don't think we're ready to know it yet. I feel very happy here and for now, that's enough for me.'

'See?' said Gideon. 'If Mia's OK, I'm OK. Just as soon as she gets nervous, I'll be wetting my pants!'

Mia laughed and went to join the group of healers and clairvoyants further down the room. Watching them grouped quietly around a large candle in the middle of the joint common room, it occurred to Dax that they might hold some answers for him. Later, when he saw her walking back in, Dax went across to Jessica Moorland. She was holding a pile of books which Dax expected would be called *Great Unexplained Myths* or *The Power From Beyond*, but on closer inspection he saw they were an annual for a pop group, Louisa M. Alcott's *Little Women*, and a skiing holidays brochure.

'Yes?' said Jennifer, looking at him curiously and raising one eyebrow. She was used to people loitering around hoping for a message from a dead relative.

'Do you ... do you ever hear from ... anyone's mum?' Dax stared at his feet and then up at her eyes, feeling very self-conscious.

Jessica's eyebrow slid back down and a look of compassion drifted on to her freckled face. She put her hand on Dax's shoulder. 'Everyone asks that,' she said, quietly. 'Every single one of us. But no, Dax. We don't ever hear. Not from our own mums or any other COLA's. It's very peculiar, but there it is.'

Dax nodded glumly. He wasn't given to dwelling on his mum, but he suddenly felt something drop a little, deep inside him. 'Your great-grandad's here though,' said Jessica, brightly. 'He says to watch where you stand.'

'Watch where I stand?' repeated Dax. He couldn't remember any of his grandparents at all.

'Yes. That's all,' said Jessica. 'If I get anything more, I'll write you out a slip. Shouldn't really be doing it now.' And she wandered off.

Gideon mooched up beside him. 'No joy on the mum front, then?' he guessed. Dax nodded sadly and Gideon smiled sympathetically and patted his shoulder. 'Never mind.'

'My great-grandad says to watch where I stand, though. What do you reckon that means?'

'Mate, if you start worrying about what it *means* every time a medium gives you a message, you'll go bonkers. There's probably a bit of Barber's poo waiting for you. Don't wear your best shoes for a while.'

14

Tregarren College assemblies took place, oddly, every Friday afternoon, just before the Friday teatime roast. This was the one occasion each week when the entire college, teachers included, sat down together to eat. One long table was erected along the top of the dining hall and draped with white damask. Candles were placed along it and lit, and the best cutlery and plates and glasses were laid out.

The students' round tables were similarly transformed and the whole college would sit down to the most sumptuous roast dinner, with perfectly cooked meat, crispy-edged roast potatoes and parsnips, stuffing, carrots, sprouts, and tangy brown gravy. A choice of delicious hot or cold puddings followed and by the end of the meal everyone was groaning with pleasure. Even the vegetarians (most of the mediums and healers were vegetarian or vegan) were well satisfied with tomato and spiced nut-roasts or mushroom and tarragon loaf.

But before the big Friday roast came the big Friday assembly. It began ordinarily enough, with singing and perhaps some literature read by one of the teachers. And then Principal Wood would stand up and give an address. He would talk, sometimes for half an hour or more, and the odd thing, thought Dax in his first assembly, was how raptly he held everyone's attention. What he was *saying* wasn't terribly interesting—it could be a series of notices about forthcoming events or a request for the telekinetics to get some of the balls off the roof of the gym. It could be a story illustrating a point that the principal wanted to make about some students' behaviour or a pep talk about learning to focus more. It didn't seem to make any difference. Principal Wood's audience was absolutely fixed upon him, even the teachers, although they at least seemed to *move* a little more, and did occasionally glance away.

Dax looked around him and saw a sea of mesmerized faces. He nudged Gideon, but his friend just went 'Shhh', and carried on gazing at Principal Wood. Dax turned back to the man on the small platform, perplexed. He moved like a cat, with an easy grace, strolling up and down and occasionally perching on the edge of a table. As he watched, Dax felt the principal's glittering eyes come to rest on him and he narrowed his gaze, trying to work out what was so *odd* about the man and, again, felt that wave of charm pulse out towards him. Then he noticed the wavering around him; a faint shimmer in the air. It was like the ground in front of the goalposts when Spook had done his illusion thing. Hang on! thought Dax, and then it came to him. Patrick Wood was using a little glamour. It was surely just vanity, but then again, who wouldn't use a touch if it meant they were assured a perfect audience? Dax grinned suddenly, wondering if anyone else had guessed the principal's secret. There was the briefest pause in the list of announcements and now the principal seemed to be scrutinizing Dax in return. Dax composed himself, and assumed an expression of deep interest, and Principal Wood resumed, with the weekly warning to the COLAs going down to the village the next day.

'If anyone—*anyone*—performs a supernatural feat, of *any degree*, then the *entire college* will be suspended from visiting Polgammon for a month. Do I make myself clear?' he concluded.

'Yes, Mr Wood,' murmured the entire audience, promptly.

He nodded and then dropped his voice to a reverential note. 'Tregarren College is something utterly extraordinary,' he said. 'It is the pinnacle of my career to be in charge of such an incredible collection of young people and there is nothing I will not do to protect Tregarren. Do you understand me?'

'Yes, Mr Wood,' came the obedient rumble.

'Good!' he beamed at them. 'Then let's eat. That smells like the finest roast yet this term!' He clapped his hands in a gesture of enthusiasm and Dax noted that at this point everyone seemed to snap out of their polite and appreciative trance. They clattered happily out of the hall and across to the dining room for their mammoth Friday roast, and not one of them seemed to be aware that they'd been charmed.

What wouldn't old Mr Clegg at Bark's End give for a

bit of *that*? thought Dax. He sat down to enjoy his meal, but a slight feeling of unease stayed with him until well after pudding.

The village of Polgammon couldn't have been prettier. Nestling into a deep, wooded cleave in the Cornish hills, its whitewashed stone cottages were roofed with dense old thatch, and lined a winding cobbled street. Thick glass windows were trimmed with late fuschias in boxes or hanging baskets. There was a general store and newsagent, a post office, a collection of gift shops which sold 'the worst tat describable to the daftest tourists imaginable' according to Gideon, the legendary chocolate parlour, and the very good fresh fish-and-chip shop.

On Dax's second Saturday, he and Gideon got a pass and went out for lunch and fresh chocolate rations. Half the school was there. Literally. You could only get a pass every *other* weekend, because the tiny village simply *couldn't* accommodate a hundred-odd pupils. Fifty or so, it could handle.

The locals were friendly with the children, but noticeably *careful*, thought Dax. They didn't engage in too much banter and never asked them how their studies were going or what they might be doing. The children, too, were careful with the locals. Nobody had forgotten the principal's regular warnings.

The chocolate parlour was everything Gideon had promised. Stocked with pound upon pound of the stuff, it seemed to offer every flavour and combination of the rich brown confectionery known to man. Gideon was in heaven as he spent his allowance on almond chocolate crunch, dark mint leaves, a heavy, dense ball of whole milk chocolate, wrapped in silver foil, and three perfect eggs, which looked completely real from the outside but were in fact made of hard sugar and lined on the inside with a creamy layer of Swiss chocolate.

Dax restricted himself to a thin, dark bar of plain chocolate, marvelling at Gideon. 'Where on earth do you put all that?'

'I don't know,' grinned Gideon, cheerily, through a mouthful of mint leaves. 'I should be Barry's size and a half, by rights. But the men in our family never put on weight.' They walked happily down the street, Gideon's pockets bulging with his purchases. He chucked the large chocolate ball up and down in one palm.

'Watch it, Reader,' said a light, jeering voice and they turned to see Spook Williams, trailing them with two friends. 'You know you mustn't display your amazing talents in public.'

Gideon caught the ball and turned to Spook, continuing their walk backwards. 'I'm *not* and you know it,' he said.

'No?' Spook suddenly darted forward and knocked the chocolate ball out of Gideon's hands and into his own. 'Well—obviously not! This is way too heavy for *you* to lift. There are ping-pong balls in the gym cupboard, you know.'

Gideon narrowed his eyes at Spook, still walking backwards, and wiped his hand angrily across his mouth. Dax took hold of his shoulder.

'Just leave it, Gid. He's trying to wind you up. Give it back, Spook,' he said evenly and the taller boy smirked.

'Or what?' he said. 'Going to turn into a fox and f-f-fwighten me?' His friends guffawed and Spook said, 'Don't worry, skin-walker. Your buddy can have his ball back. Here you go, Reader. Catch!'

He threw the chocolate globe high into the air. It soared, like a small UFO, too far away for Gideon to run for it. Gideon shouted and Dax saw his face swiftly move into focus, ready to gain control of the plummeting sphere and then, within a split second, the boy had collected himself and dropped his gaze, furiously, to the floor. The ball of chocolate smashed heavily into the road and silver and dark brown splinters flew off in all directions. Gideon raised a livid face to Spook and the boy, laughing uproariously, darted between his friends and ran back up the village street, calling back, 'Oh, help! Help! Freckles and Foxy are cross with me!'

'Gideon! Don't bother!' Dax bawled after him and then ran along in his wake.

'There's no rule,' yelled back Gideon, 'about *not* punching Spook's teeth out!'

He was a fast runner and was soon gaining on Spook. Dax could make out the taller boy, haring up the road past the last two village shops. As he reached the crest of the hill, Gideon hot on his heels, Dax saw

Spook suddenly drop into the road, and heard a howl of pain echo down the street. Gideon reached him and then drew up, without launching into a fist frenzy as Dax had been fully expecting. Dax caught up a few seconds later to find a small crowd of COLAs gathering around Spook, who was writhing around by a loose kerbstone, apparently in agony.

'My ankle! I've broken my ankle,' he gasped, and indeed, the colour was draining from his face and he yelled out in pain when Gideon attempted to shift his leg out of the road and onto the pavement. 'Get your hands off me, Gideon,' he hissed and then moaned and tried to look at his ankle.

'You'll all need to gather round close, or someone might see,' said a warm, calm voice, and the crowd parted to let Mia through. She knelt down beside Spook and said, 'Are you still with us?' Spook nodded, but even the blood from his lips had drained away now. Nobody doubted that his ankle was broken and about eight COLAs now huddled round him, while others scattered out wider, keeping watch. 'Are we clear?' asked Mia, coolly, like a surgeon.

'Yes,' said several voices.

'OK, look at me, Spook.' Spook had been screwing up his eyes but he forced them open and looked into Mia's. She smiled her amazing smile and put both hands on to Spook's ankle.

Dax watched, fascinated, as her eyelids drooped a little and she seemed to be gazing at something that the rest of them couldn't see. Spook's anguished groans quietened and his breathing evened out. A minute passed and Mia's face remained in its sleepy, half smiling position. At last her eyes shifted and she seemed to see the rest of them again. She released Spook's ankle and knelt up. 'All done?' she said to him.

He stared back at her, the colour now returning to his face. He shifted his leg carefully and shook his head in amazement. 'Fine,' he said, and began to get up. 'Absolutely fine!' He smiled, without a trace of his usual mockery, for a change, and thanked his classmate profusely.

'Go! Go now!' someone said, urgently, and Dax craned round to see two villagers heading up the road, giving the small crowd nervy glances. Everyone spread out and walked off in all directions.

'Won't she get into trouble?' Dax asked Gideon, as he watched Mia and Jennifer head back down the hill.

'Only if someone tells, and nobody will,' said Gideon. 'Everyone loves Mia, even Spook—and he usually only loves himself. Didn't you see the way he looked at her?'

But Dax was watching Mia again. She had walked down the hill and then paused and was now leaning against one of the low, whitewashed stone walls. She was smiling and holding her hands up to Jennifer. Then she stood up and walked on, but Dax noticed that she had a very, very slight limp.

As the days wore on and Dax grew more and more

comfortable at COLA Club, only one thing really troubled him: his complete inability to turn into a fox. He felt like a fraud. Everyone around him was doing spectacular things on an almost daily basis: Gideon was working hard on floating heavier and heavier objects and could now keep a pillow steady in the air for up to three minutes; Barry was trying to control his breathing so he could stay invisible without being found; Jessica Moorland and her medium friends were forever handing out pink Spirit Communication Notices; and Lisa was still wandering around looking so permanently angry and tired that clearly there was no let-up in her clairvoyant powers, no matter how badly she wished for it.

But Dax was just, well, Dax. True, he was resistant to glamour, and was noticing this more and more, but it hardly felt like a *power*. It felt more like being left out of a fun game. In the dining hall on Wednesday, Spook Williams and Fred Chaucer had the whole school in fits with a walking table mirage, sending a table full of lunch strolling around the room and apparently whistling to itself and occasionally burping. With everyone—even the dinner ladies—hooting with laughter, all Dax could see was Spook and Fred, standing up and focusing hard in the direction of the table in question, and a slight wavering in the air. He had to laugh anyway and try to follow everyone else's gaze, because he wanted to keep his glamour resistance to himself and Gideon and Barry. He understood that it really *was* a power; a protection that meant that he couldn't be fully charmed. Nevertheless, it added to his feeling of being sadly lacking compared to his classmates.

He'd had two further Development Sessions. One with Owen which went much the same way as before and ended in another urgent count-back to bring him back to full consciousness, gasping and shouting. The second session was with Mr Eades, the dull, dry little man who almost never looked Dax in the eye, with Paulina Sartre observing. Mr Eades had simply sat him down in B12 at a table opposite him and tested his psychic powers, holding up cards with images turned away from Dax, and asking him what he thought they were. Dax's answers clearly didn't impress him much. He scored thirty-two per cent.

So, as time passed, Dax began to wonder whether it had all been a mistake. Owen seemed to pick up his fear. 'Don't worry, Dax,' he'd said, after the second hypnosis session, as they left Mr Eades in B12 and walked back up the underground corridor. 'It will come. You will learn how to make it happen. It just takes time.'

'Maybe it was just a temporary thing,' muttered Dax forlornly.

'No,' said Owen, firmly. 'It's still there, inside you. It's there for a reason.'

Dax pondered this. He hadn't thought about any particular *reason* for his strange ability.

'But . . . what if it was just a fluke? Maybe . . . maybe that *other* kid should really have been the one,' he said, remembering the other shapeshifter who'd died, that Owen had mentioned during their first proper talk in the lorry. 'What—what exactly happened with the other one?'

Owen paused at the bottom of the stairwell, looking grave. 'He was up in Scotland,' he said. 'And he was changing into a wolf. It was about a year ago.' He sighed and shook his head. 'We took too long to get to him.' His eyes had the look of a man who was still seeing something he'd rather not have seen.

'Patrick Wood and I went to get him, but something went wrong. We spoke to him and we made the arrangements and then, while Patrick was bringing him back across town, he shifted, for some reason, right in the middle of a crowd. It was mad—stupid. Patrick said people were screaming and chasing him like something out of mediaeval times. Then he got up to the A-road before we could stop him.'

Dax gulped. 'How did he die?'

'Hit by a truck, we think. We'll never know for sure. Patrick found him first, on the verge, still a wolf. They don't do autopsies on wild animals; not even exotic escaped pets—which is what they decided he was.'

Dax stared at the floor, imagining that bleak scene. 'What about his family? What did you tell them?'

'He didn't have a family,' said Owen. 'He was in a children's home. What could we tell them? There was no proof. Just a dead wolf.'

'He didn't change back then?'

'No. He didn't have time. They say if you're killed instantly by a shot or a blow to the head while you're in a different form, you die as that form. It's only if you're still conscious as you die that you shift back again. That's what I've read, anyway.' Owen began walking up the stairs. 'He's still classified as a missing person—and with kids in care it's not that unusual. Enough of this, though, Dax. That was his story—not yours. You're safe, and, heaven be praised, you're not a wolf.'

Owen's revelations didn't do much to ease Dax's mind. He still felt unsure about whether his powers would ever return. Maybe they'd send him home at the end of term. This unhappy thought was troubling him on the Sunday night after Spook's broken ankle incident, as he lay in bed watching raindrops pelting into the sloping window over his head and scudding down the glass. Gideon and Barry were asleep and Dax sighed heavily to himself. He was going to have to come up with the answer to this— but what *was* it? He couldn't force himself into a panic every time he wanted to change, and he certainly didn't want to choke himself with Triple Eight, the substance Owen had mentioned, which he guessed was the vapour stuff he'd used on him in the lorry. There *must* be another way.

Dax decided to try the hypnosis thing on himself. He deepened his breathing and began the scrunching up and relaxing business that Owen had taught him. It worked well and he found himself drifting comfortably down under the first layer of sleep, his breathing measured and deep, and yet his brain quite alert. He sent himself back to the sunny, warm wood above the college and lay there for a while, gently poking around in his mind for clues as to how to move *on* from here. He didn't want to imagine the horrible hot shed all over again; he'd really had enough of that, but something in the *smell* came to him, not of the ghastly white spirit, but the smell he'd picked up *before* all that began.

It *was* that hot sharp stink of fox that he'd noticed first; a smell that both repelled and attracted him; a smell that spoke of *earth*. Deep, deep earth. A smell that made you think you could press your face into the ground and feel the turning of the world on its axis across your brow, that you could reach in and touch the hot, thrumming core of the planet you were clinging to, that you could sink down into the soil as if it was a warm bath and admit that you were *part* of it and not just trotting about, detached, on its crust.

Dax took in a deep, shuddering breath and felt a warmth curling around his arms and waist and legs and forehead. A sense of being lightly brushed with cool air then passed from the very crown of his head, right down his body and to the tips of his paws. Dax curled into the quilt, feeling the cotton pucker and move with him. As he stretched his limbs, reawakening the fluid, fox muscles, a huge, happy yawn stretched his jaws and the quilt cover blew up in a small tent over his snout. He was completely buried in it, and as he dug his way back out to his pillow and stood lightly up on the edge of the bed, his tail raised and his ears aloft, he was assailed with a feeling of utter joy. He'd *done* it! He'd done it himself!

15

Dax's claws clipped daintily across the dormitory floor as he trotted to the door. He had to go up on his hind legs to push down the handle, which flipped awkwardly a couple of times before the latch disengaged and the door eased open. The rain on the roof seemed to be easing off, he noticed, his sharp ears aware of every sound. Good. It was time to go out.

He walked quietly down the corridor and then easily negotiated the spiral staircase in the lounge. He was relieved to find it dark and empty. It was after midnight, but it wasn't unusual to find COLAs having a wander or distracting themselves with overnight DVDs.

Outside, the rain clouds were beginning to clear and a full moon was lighting the little stone paths around the college. Dax paused and wondered where to go. He looked up at the cliff above the dorm, which was crowned at the very top by the edge of the wood he and Gideon had visited. He badly wanted to get back to the wood. (But *no* spiders! he told himself, although he was already feeling hungry.) He stared at the cliffside. It was too steep for a boy to climb—but what about a fox? From where he stood he thought he could trace a path, a route from outcrop to weed clump, to another outcrop . . . perhaps it *was* possible. Dax skirted the dorms and located the start of this path, behind the girls' block. His deft paws found the climbing points and he began to ascend with little leaps and scrambles, thinking that at any moment he would have to stop and turn back, but he was thrilled to find himself at the top, his paws resting on the gnarled roots at the edge, in no time at all.

Dax plunged into the wood and his head was at once flooded with information. There were mice and voles tickling the ground around him, earthworms curling up to catch the residue of the rain shower, a badger—he didn't know how he knew, but he did: it was the smell—was foraging among the worms somewhere off to his left, and at least three owls were on the hunt. He could hear the 'q-wick' of the tawny and the answering hoot of her mate and *felt* the ghostlike passing of a barn owl, scanning the earth for prey. He also sensed the reaction of the creatures around him as he moved through the dark wood. They tensed and waited and some scurried away. Only the owls and the badger were untroubled, although the owls were wary.

Dax jumped. Literally bounded into the air, so full he was of elastic joy. He bounded and bounded until he found himself in a small clearing and then something pulsed into his head. *Warning.* That's what it said. It wasn't a scary experience, it was actually quite a reasonable signal, but very firm. Dax turned round to see, some ten metres away, another *fox*. He stood rooted to the ground, thrilled. Could he *talk* to another fox?

Could it talk to him? The dog-fox regarded him from the top of a fallen log. It jumped lightly down, paused, and then walked towards him, sniffing the air and eyeing him suspiciously. Then it cocked its back leg and marked the log. The pungent scent rose up into the air and Dax got the message. This is *my* terrain. He sensed that the dog-fox preferred *not* to fight him, but clearly he would, if Dax were to advance any further. Dax stepped back, to indicate his willingness to respect the dog-fox's rights, but he *so* wanted to wait awhile; to see if he could possibly communicate with it.

'Can you understand me?' he said, in his head.

The fox just stood his ground, staring Dax down. Dax tried to *speak* the words and let out a series of barks and light, unmenacing growls as he repeated his thought aloud. The dog-fox jumped and advanced two or three steps, its ears pricked and its black snout high, looking surprised but not frightened. Again it sent out *Warning!* Dax realized that he wasn't going to get a chat with this one. The last thing he needed on his first self-induced outing was a scrap with another fox. He nodded his head and turned away. He was aware of the creature's relief and a little triumph as he padded quickly back through the trees, retracing his path. When he glanced over his shoulder, the dog-fox was gone.

As he reached the edge of the cliff, Dax gazed down at the college. He loved this place. And he felt so, so, *so* much better about being here, now that he'd *made* himself be a fox. But hunger was starting to get to him again—*why* was he *always* hungry when he was a fox? More tempting rustles in the tree bark and leaf litter attracted his attention. Mmmm . . . how about a little earthworm snack? NO! Dax the boy countered firmly. No to worms, no to spiders and no . . . his eyes lit upon a juicy black beetle clambering across a twig right under his nose and, before he could hold himself back, his fox instinct overpowered him and he'd snapped it up and was cracking its shell between his sharp teeth. It was warm and slightly sweet and gone in a second. That's *it*! snapped Dax the boy, horrified. Get back to the college *now*. He scanned the pathway back down the cliff, which didn't look anywhere near as inviting on the downward route, and began carefully picking his way back down.

But as he reached the first outcrop, something in the distance caught his eye. Far out on the playing field, just visible in a gap between the dormitory buildings and the joint common room, someone was running. Running alone in the moonlight. Dax stared. It wasn't a desperate kind of run. It was measured and even and the runner was skirting the pitch with an easy, practised gait. Curious, Dax skipped back down the dangerously steep cliff, leaping from pawhold to pawhold without a thought and set off down the winding path, tail held high, towards the field, fascinated to find out who the midnight runner could be.

The sea breeze rippled through his fur as he headed across the promontory and on to the edge of the pitch. Keeping low to the ground and in the shadow of the fence, Dax paused and scrutinized the figure as it reached the far corner of the grass. The girl was wearing proper running shorts and a sleek zip-up running top and her trainers looked expensive. It was Lisa Hardman. She was moving fluidly and fast and looked more relaxed and contented than Dax had ever seen her.

As she neared his corner, Dax rose up and wandered across her path, and she drew to a surprised halt. Wonder crept over her face and for the first time, Dax saw her smile. She knelt down and held out her hand, still breathing fast from her exercise. Dax trotted over to her, as intrigued about the girl as she was about the fox. He touched his nose delicately into her palm and she gasped, delighted, and then stroked the top of his furry head. Resting back on her heels, Lisa lowered her head and looked him hard in the eyes. 'Dax?' she breathed. 'Is that you?'

He remembered what Gideon had said about all their secrets getting out. Of course, everyone would know by now. Dax chuckled and it came out as a raspy little bark and he nodded his head. It was fantastic to be recognized now, now that it was safe.

'Wow!' said Lisa. Her blonde hair was up in a ponytail, and it flipped from side to side as she shook her head. 'This is amazing! Can you talk?' Dax shook his head. 'Try it in your head,' she urged. 'I might be able to understand you.'

Of course, thought Dax, she had powers! She was clairaudient and clairvoyant and all that, so she might well be able to read his thoughts too.

'I can pick up some of it,' she responded. 'But it's a bit jumbled at the moment. Concentrate on what you want to say to me and keep it simple. Tell me what you had for supper.'

Dax remembered he'd eaten hot tomato soup with a crusty roll and butter.

'Soup and a roll?' checked Lisa and he nodded, jumping up onto his feet in delight. 'Brilliant!' shouted Lisa, clapping her hands. It was good to see her looking so happy.

'What are you doing, running around the field in the middle of the night?' asked Dax, in his head.

Lisa stood up, looking around her edgily. 'Run with me for a bit. I'll tell you as we go,' she said and jogged off again. Dax easily kept up with her. 'I've always loved running,' said Lisa as they went. 'It clears my head and makes me feel alive. I used to run for my school back home.' She pressed her lips together for a moment and they ran on in silence as she struggled with her homesickness. 'Anyway, it's good for me. It helps to keep them off me. They wouldn't let me sleep, so I came out. I'm out here at least a couple of nights every week. I don't know why, but when I'm running I don't get so much stuff coming through, and anything that *does* come through isn't so bad. Sometimes it's even quite nice.'

They ran on without speaking for a few seconds and then Dax asked, 'So what's happening to you? Why are you always so upset?'

'How would you feel?' she said, defensively. 'Imagine

you're sitting down, quite happy, watching a good programme on TV—and then, all of a sudden, the channel just changes itself and you're looking at something really grim or mad or scary, or just completely dumb, so you haven't a clue what it's supposed to be or what it means.'

Lisa speeded up her run, breathing harder and faster, and glancing back over her shoulder as if she were being chased. Luckily, Dax had no problem keeping up; he could have lapped the field three times faster if he'd wanted. But all he wanted was to hear what else Lisa was going to say.

'I started getting these stupid channel changes— messages and visions and stuff—about a year ago. I thought I was going mad. Then, when people at school or at home lost something, I always—*always*—knew where it was. I stopped telling people in the end, because they started to think I was stealing their things and hiding them. I mean, how else could I know? At school they started to treat me like a freak, and then,' she gulped and her mouth drew in tight again, as she struggled against some wave of emotion, 'and then this girl came in one day, and there was a funny grey cloud all around her. Nobody else could see it, of course, and I wasn't stupid enough to say anything, but it made me so scared and so—so *sad*. I knew what was going to happen, you see. I knew it—but I couldn't *stop* it—so what was the point? What was the point?'

She stumbled to a halt and turned round to look searchingly down at Dax. He stopped too, and sat back, curling his tail around his paws and waiting. He didn't want to egg her on to find out what happened. He could see that thinking about it was terribly upsetting. But Lisa sank down, cross-legged, on to the grass and rested her elbows on her knees and her face in her hands. After a moment she lifted her head, and spoke hollowly.

'First, there would be a sound, like a roar and a metallic sort of shriek, then an immense thud—a crunch—then there'd be a smell of hot oil and cold tarmac and there would be little diamonds, raining down, sparkling in the sunlight, falling and falling and twinkling in the sun. The diamonds were beautiful.' Tears were now streaming down Lisa's face. 'Really, really beautiful. I like—I like to think about those being the last thing that . . . I like to think . . . ' Lisa's words trailed off and she pulled out a hanky and blew her nose and rested her head back in her palms again for a while.

Dax was horrified. He walked over to her and put a paw on her knee.

'She died,' she said, in a resigned, thin voice. 'In a road accident, later that week. The car she got hit by had its windscreen shattered in the impact and there were little bits of glass everywhere.'

Dax didn't know what to say. How awful. How completely horrible. Who could ever say that a power like that was a *gift*?

'So, anyway,' said Lisa, sniffing and getting back to her feet, 'it's been like that ever since. More visions and messages and interference from people I don't even *know.*

It doesn't matter what I say or do—it all just keeps coming. And I ask you—what am I supposed to do? I *have* said something to people, once or twice. Complete strangers who looked at me like I was a lunatic. I don't know if anything I said made any difference. Whether they found something that they really needed, or whether they went and had a check-up and got their disease healed before it got them, I don't know and I don't care. I just want it to stop. So most of the time I don't do *anything* any more. I reckon they'll all give up on me sooner or later and go and find someone who *wants* to be gifted.'

'But maybe,' said Dax, still talking in his head, trotting alongside her as she broke back into a run, 'maybe if you started telling people, or even writing out SCN slips and posting them or something, maybe they'd lay off you for a while.'

Lisa ran on, looking sceptical. She stopped by the path that led back to the dorms and looked at him, considering.

'The trouble is, I'm close to making the college think that I'm not really of any use,' she said. 'If I keep it up they might send me back home.'

'But it's not about you being of *use*,' said Dax. 'It's about you being safe and looked after.'

Lisa looked at him with a pitying expression. 'Yeah, right,' she said. 'Like they're going to send us all off with a party bag when we turn eighteen!'

'But it won't make any difference whether you're here or not, don't you see?' insisted Dax. 'Your messages and visions will still keep on coming. At least *here* you might be able to learn a way of blocking them out. I'm sure Mr Hind could help with that. Why don't you talk to him?'

'No,' she said stubbornly. 'I won't talk to him. It was talking to some stupid psychiatrist that got me here in the first place. My dad *made* me and now I'm stuck here!'

'But it's *great* here!' said Dax.

'For *you* maybe. But look—Dax—perhaps I could tell you things, sometimes, that you could pass on? You needn't say they were messages from *me*. That way, if anything can be done, then I've helped a bit. But I'm not going overboard!'

'But I thought you said you weren't going to go along with it,' said Dax, puzzled.

'I *know* what I said,' she snapped. 'But—but sometimes it gets so bad . . . '

'OK,' said Dax. 'Go on then. Can you tell me one now?'

Lisa sighed and leaned against the girls' dormitory door. She screwed up her face and Dax saw weariness and misery steal across it in waves. 'All right! All *right*!' she said, through gritted teeth. 'Back *off*! I don't need to see it again. I'm going to tell him.' Dax felt the fur stand up on the back of his neck. It was seriously eerie to see her in conversation with some spirit. She opened her eyes and said, dully, 'His name is Stephen Seabright. He's stuck on a ledge below the Roche Rocks on Bodmin Moor. He says his family are desperate and they really need to find him.'

'And you've been keeping this to yourself?!' asked Dax, aghast.

Lisa eyed him stonily. 'It's not like there's any point in hurrying,' she said. 'He's dead.'

16

Gideon was beaming at Dax, sitting up in bed with his arms and legs folded, his smile reaching from ear to ear. Dax sat up groggily.

'What?' he said.

'You've been and gone and done it, haven't you?' said Gideon. 'Mate—you could have woken me up! You could have let me come with you!'

Dax was confused. When he'd slipped quietly back into the dorm last night and curled once under the quilt before dropping off to sleep, he had been quite certain that Gideon and Barry were still asleep.

'How did you do it?' urged Gideon, leaning forward with fascination. He knew Dax had been struggling to shift again.

'How did you know?' yawned Dax, sitting up and rubbing his eyes. 'You were both fast asleep.'

Gideon pointed to the floor and across it Dax saw a neat set of muddy fox-prints that led to his bed. Looking down he saw more traces of the soggy sports field on his sheets. Oops. The laundry staff weren't going to be impressed about *that*. Then Dax remembered his transformation last night and a huge, delighted grin spread across his face.

'Sorry, Gideon,' he said. 'I'll wake you up next time. It was just so—amazing! And I needed to get used to it on my own for a bit.'

On the way down to breakfast, Dax told Gideon about his climb up to the wood and his encounter with the dog-fox. He confessed to eating the beetle, which made Gideon howl with delight and jump up and down, biting his knuckle and making disgusted faces. He didn't, though, tell him about his meeting with Lisa. She hadn't exactly sworn him to secrecy, but he felt that it had been private. Maybe he'd tell Gideon in due course. Gideon had become his best friend and he wasn't comfortable keeping anything from him.

'But how did you manage to *do* it?' asked Gideon, keeping his voice down as they approached the dining room and other students.

'I'm not exactly sure, but I was trying to do that hypnosis thing that Mr Hind taught me. I think maybe being on my own made a difference. I mean, that Mr Eades has been there the last two times I've tried in Development—and . . . and somebody else.' Dax thought, fleetingly, of the sense that somebody unseen was also in B12. 'I think I might have made it if it was just Mr Hind there, but Mr Eades gives me the creeps.'

'Me too,' said Gideon. 'He always looks like someone's just put cold porridge down his pants.' The boys snorted and wandered in to breakfast, laughing.

It was one of the mornings when the principal made an appearance. From time to time, Mr Wood chose to eat breakfast with his students. He would start on one table with his cereal, then gather up his tray and move to another table with his toast and finally shift once more to yet another table, to finish his coffee. He was generally made welcome. The children found him interesting and enigmatic and liked to have discussions with him.

Dax watched him talking to Barry and Jennifer, a table along from them, as the principal buttered his toast and asked Barry to pass the marmalade. 'Gideon,' he asked, 'do you like Mr Wood?'

'Yeah. He's cool,' said Gideon, attacking his sausages with gusto. He didn't look up.

'Why?'

'What do you mean?'

'What is it about him that's cool? Why do you like him?'

Gideon looked across at Mr Wood and then back at Dax, perplexed. 'Well,' he said, 'he's . . . he's . . . I don't know. He's just sort of . . . '

'Charming?' said Dax.

'Yeah. That's it,' said Gideon, going back to his sausages. 'Why? Don't *you* like him?'

'I like him fine,' said Dax.

He didn't add his second thought; that he didn't entirely *trust* the principal. Dax felt unsure of the degree of mistrust he had for Mr Wood. Was it just that he knew, and perhaps nobody else did, that the man used a little glamour to make people like him more? There was nothing wrong with that, surely. Although, Dax thought, it didn't seem entirely *honest*. People should like you for what you were, not for what you *seemed* to be. But then, didn't everyone, even ordinary people, *try* to appear cleverer or more interesting than they really were from time to time? Dax shrugged off the tiny seed of unease inside him and decided that, on balance, if Gideon liked Mr Wood, and everyone else liked him, he was probably misreading the man. He would like him, too, and that was that.

At this point, the principal finished his last slice of toast and marmalade, said cheerio to Barry and Jennifer, and brought his tray across to sit with Gideon and Dax. 'Morning, boys,' he said with a friendly smile, before cupping his mug of coffee in his hands and taking a gulp. 'How are you liking Tregarren College, Dax? Gideon looking after you?'

'It's fantastic,' said Dax, warmly. 'I love it here. And Gideon's been brilliant.'

'Good to see you both getting on so well together,' said Mr Wood, and drained his coffee quickly. Dax thought he'd get up and head off, but he stayed seated and said, 'Gideon—would you mind getting me a refill?' He held up his empty mug.

'Of course not, sir,' said Gideon, and Dax thought he sounded odd, as if he was *really* trying to impress. This was not like Gideon. Gideon was usually trying to be cool.

The principal steepled his fingers together, resting his elbows on the table and regarding Dax with his odd, glittery eyes. Dax found it very hard to swallow his boiled egg and toast soldiers. He looked up at the man and felt, again, that odd *pulse*. With a shiver, he realized that Mr Wood was making a concerted effort to charm him. But what should he do? How should he react? He didn't want the man to suspect that he was resistant. Dax saw Gideon returning with the principal's refilled cup of coffee and noted the rather daft, eager look on his face. *That* was it! Dax put down his spoon and beamed up at Mr Wood, copying exactly the look on Gideon's face. The principal sat back in his chair immediately, his shoulders relaxing, and cheerfully accepted the cup from Gideon. He didn't push a charm on to Dax again, as they chatted about how the Tregarren Tigers were doing against the Terrors, and how much weight Gideon was now able to lift with his mind. Dax relaxed, too. Maybe he'd convinced the principal. He must be careful and try to blend more with the others if he didn't want to excite the man's suspicion again.

After breakfast, in the few minutes before classes began, Dax sought out Owen. He found him just leaving his cob dwelling in the cliff and threading his way down through the zigzag stone paths.

'Hello, Dax,' said Owen, warmly. 'How's it going?'

Dax had to stop himself hopping up and down with pleasure as he broke the news. 'I *think* I've worked out how to do it,' he said, grinning joyfully. The unexpected happiness that he'd felt in the night was still lapping around him, buoying him up.

Owen stopped on the steps and looked at him closely. 'You've made yourself change?' Dax nodded, bouncing about excitedly on the balls of his feet.

'Dax, that's fantastic! Excellent! How did you trigger it? What made the difference?'

Dax told him about his self-hypnosis and all that had followed, up until he'd noticed Lisa on the sports field. He left that out, because he had promised to keep her name out of it. But as he finished his story and enjoyed the delight in Owen's face, he knew he had to pass on the message.

'Look, there's something *else* I have to tell you,' he said. 'Someone's told me about something, which they can't tell themselves.' Owen's delighted expression settled into curiosity and mild concern. 'They need—*I* need—to pass on a message.'

'Is it a spirit communication?' asked Owen matter-of-factly.

'Yes. There's a man called Stephen Seabright. He's—he's dead, I think.' Owen nodded. 'He's lying on a ledge below somewhere called Roche Rocks? On Bodmin Moor?' Owen nodded again. 'His family needs to know where he is,' said Dax. 'That's all. They need to know.'

'OK,' said Owen. 'I'll get the message out. Thanks, Dax. One of the less pleasant duties of our clairvoyants and mediums, I'm afraid.' Dax turned to head on down to class. 'Dax,' called Owen, and Dax paused on the steps, squinting back up at him in the early morning sun. 'Perhaps you could tell your friend that she—or he—can

168

come and talk to me, whenever they like? That I can probably help?'

'I did,' said Dax, with a nod. 'I will again.'

The next time he saw Lisa was at the woodsman class that Owen had arranged at 3 o'clock, after school that day. They all met up at the gate tower: Dax, Gideon, Mia, and Lisa. Dax was surprised, but quite glad, that there weren't more students taking up Owen's offer. He tried to talk to Lisa, quietly, but she turned away as if she hadn't heard and ignored him completely, as if nothing at all had happened last night.

Fine! thought Dax, peeved. Lisa stayed close to Mia, putting off all chances of a private discussion, so Dax returned to Gideon and resolved to try later—just once. He wasn't going to bend over backwards if she was going to be like that.

It didn't feel remotely *like* a class; it was more of an expedition. They were all in jeans and thick jumpers and their boots and trainers thudded across the round wooden floor of the gate tower as Mr Pengalleon counted them through after a friendly chat with Owen.

'You pay close attention, now,' he instructed them as he decoded and opened the outer door. 'There's not many that can teach you more than Mr Hind.' And he gave Owen a fond pat on the shoulder, while Barber wove himself between their legs, his tail thumping happily.

Dax smiled to himself as they entered the wood. It was only this morning—*very early* this morning—that he'd trodden, much more lightly, on the same ground. Owen flashed him a grin, and he guessed the man was reading his thoughts.

'OK, everyone.' Owen halted the small party under the trees close to some dense undergrowth. 'We'll start with the basics. One of the most useful things you can learn in a wood is how to make yourself a shelter.'

They looked at each other, surprised. They had been expecting a lesson in whittling or identifying trees. Owen unsheathed a knife from his thick leather belt and held it up, glinting, in a shaft of sunlight that fell between the branches overhead.

'You'll need a knife, and this is one of the best kind you can get, although you may find it hard to buy at a shop, until you're a bit older.' The knife had a sturdy wooden handle and a steel blade which curved to a well-sharpened point on one side. Owen handed it to Gideon and said, 'Pass it around—*carefully*—it's very sharp.' And each of them took hold of it and gingerly touched the point to a finger. Mia handed it back to Owen.

'I've got a Swiss Army Knife,' said Gideon and hooked the chunky red folding tool out of his pocket, opening out the scissors and the file proudly.

'They can be very handy,' said Owen. 'But they're not ideal for working with wood. The blade can get caught and fold back in on your fingers if you're not careful.' Gideon put the knife back into his pocket.

'With a good, strong knife, and with a little guidance and patience, you can create an excellent shelter in habitat like this,' went on Owen. 'But if you get caught out without a knife, you can still use what's around you, if you know where to look. We'll start with the best kind of shelter for woodland like this. A leaf hut. OK—first stand still, look up and listen. Check for dead branches above you that might fall—a creaking noise is a give-away. People have been killed in their sleep by deadfalls.'

They all peered up into the canopy, but it just hissed and murmured at them in the breeze and there was no sign of any danger.

'You'd be fine here,' said Owen, at length. 'Now—I need you all to collect some long sticks and branches. See what's on the wood floor, but also let me know if there are low lying, attached branches which would serve us well. They need to be at least as high as your chest in length. Hazel is always good.'

The group happily split up and began searching through the undergrowth for suitable sticks. In half an hour they had gathered a pile of them, mostly from the wood floor, but some from trees which Owen had cut off, demonstrating with his knife; cutting cleanly and away from the body, with confident strokes. He then showed them all how to cut the unwanted shoots and twigs off the branches.

'Always cut away from the body, to the side,' he said, as Lisa took the knife. 'And never work the wood across your legs. If you slip with your knife, you could sever your femoral artery—and bleed to death. Keep your thumb back behind the guard on the shaft. Don't try to rest it along the blade.'

Owen chose the three stoutest branches and, getting Dax and Lisa to help, drove them into the earth and angled the forked ends towards each other. They met and knotted in together, creating the framework for the structure. Owen lay down on the earth beneath them and was able to stretch out straight inside. Getting up, he got them all to start laying the lesser branches and sticks up against the frame, in a rough lattice. When they were all heaped around two sides of the frame, leaving the third open, the structure began to take shape, like a small, woody cave or half a short wigwam.

'OK—leaves now,' said Owen and they all set to with leaves and peat and litter from the wood floor, until the shelter walls and roof were completely covered. It was hugely rewarding. From one side, the shelter rose up in a leafy, twiggy knoll, looking just like a natural hump on the wood floor. Around the front, however, was an opening into a small, curved shelter. Even Lisa was grinning. Her expensive jeans and jumper were smudged with dirt and leaf, but she was completely unaware of it.

'Can we get in?' she asked enthusiastically and they all started forward.

'Hang on,' said Owen, wiping his dirty hands on a handkerchief. 'Go get some of that first.'

He pointed to a lush green lake of bracken a short sprint away and everyone dashed across to it with little whoops and leaps of excitement. They gathered armfuls of the large, elegant leaves, and rushed back to create a cool green bed inside the shelter. Then they all jammed into it, sitting tightly in together and giggling. Owen pulled a few leaves of bracken back out and sat down outside, peering in at them and enjoying their delight.

'Bracken is good for a temporary seat,' he said, 'but don't sleep on it unless it's brown and dead. The green stuff won't insulate you properly while you sleep—it'll actually make you colder. Go for dry spruce boughs or heather instead if you can get them.'

He picked up his bag and rummaged inside it, and pulled out a flask and a stack of plastic mugs. He decanted a hot torrent of cocoa into each mug and handed them in to his small, pleased class, and they cooed with appreciation. Owen sat back on his leaves and enjoyed his own hot drink. Dax was warmed through, not just with the cocoa, but with the feeling of the *best* people, all around him.

'Come on, time to break camp and go home,' said Owen, at length, and they realized that the light was beginning to fade fast. 'You've done well. Will you be able to remember this, and how we did it?' Everyone was sure they would. Owen nodded, as if this was very important to him. 'Good. Now—take it down.'

They looked at him in dismay. 'Take it down?' howled Gideon. 'But we've only just made it!'

'Can't we leave it for someone else?' pleaded Mia, but Owen shook his head firmly.

'No. First rule of bushlore. You don't leave any trace of your camp once you've moved on, if you can possibly help it. Come on—help me take it down.'

With moans and complaints, they did as they were told,

pulling and kicking at the shelter until it was flattened, and then scattering the wood around beneath the trees. In minutes, their two hours of work had vanished.

As he threw one of the last few sticks away into the undergrowth, Owen gave a sudden curse, and bent to pull up his trousers at the ankle. He'd stepped into a patch of viciously barbed brambles, and there was a red tear across his skin. Mia crossed to him quickly and went to drop down and touch the wound but, oddly, Owen held her off. 'No,' he said, quietly, but firmly, and Mia stood back up, looking surprised and a little hurt. The others were a little way off, and Dax wasn't close, but his hearing, which was getting sharper and sharper it seemed, picked up their short exchange.

'I can make it better,' said Mia, simply.

Owen stood up straight, ignoring his bloodied ankle and said again, more firmly still, 'No. It's *my* pain, Mia. You don't need to take it away. You don't need to. Do you understand?'

Mia gave him a strange, shaky sort of smile, and turned to join the others. Nothing else was said, but she was very quiet on the way back to the college. Lost in her own thoughts, she wandered ahead of Lisa, which gave Dax the chance, finally, to talk about the message.

'I passed it on,' he said, quietly, as he caught Lisa up. She didn't slow down or look at him.

'I know,' she said.

'How do you know?' asked Dax.

'Because Stephen Seabright's finally stopped shouting in my ear.'

They walked on in silence, although Dax was just about to tell her that she *could* say thank you, when she suddenly gasped 'Oh!' and stopped in her tracks. The others were walking ahead and didn't seem to notice. Lisa shook her head and resumed her walking. 'That's a first,' Dax heard her mutter to herself.

'What?' asked Dax, curiously, in spite of his annoyance with her.

'An animal spirit, for crying out loud,' she said, pulling a sarcastic face. 'It's bad enough with all the human ones whining at me. I'm not starting up a zoo!'

'What kind of animal?' he asked.

'Doesn't matter,' she said, flicking her hair back carelessly. 'I'm not paying any attention.'

'Oh go on—which?'

Lisa sighed. 'I told you I don't like talking about it. It was a wolf. Now just drop it, OK?'

She ran to catch up with Mia and Dax stood still. The hairs on his arms and the back of his neck bristled and a cold chill swept through him. In the same moment he thought of the other shapeshifter, lying dead at the roadside, Patrick Wood beside it and Owen approaching. And a feeling came to him that he didn't like.

Up ahead, Gideon turned. 'Keep up, Daxy boy!'

Dax shook himself out of his uneasy reverie and ran to catch his friend. He told himself to forget it—like Gideon said, if he took seriously everything a passing medium said, he'd go bonkers.

17

Dax began to wonder how he'd ever lived without COLA Club. Now that he'd found the key to controlling his shapeshifting, he felt more and more part of the college. In the company of people who cared about him, he worked happily at his studies, and for the first time began to find himself among the top students.

It still amazed him that he—and all the other students—could continue to study in the midst of almost continuous reminders of their incredible powers. Banned from displaying them as they were in everyday lessons, it was still quite acceptable to chat about how high you'd levitated yesterday; that you'd been exchanging views with Chopin during Monday's seance session; or that you were exhausted after pulverizing a dinner lady's gallstones, with the healing power of your *thoughts*.

And, of course, there was the endless postal round of little pink SCN slips. Gideon got one from his Auntie Pam at least once a week, although she never seemed to say anything of note. 'Eat more beans' had been the last ominous message from beyond the grave. It wasn't like in the films . . .

Once, Dax had thought *he* was about to get a pink slip, because Jessica Moorland had been striding down the corridor towards him, smiling meaningfully, with something pink and fluttery in her palm, but just then she'd been called away by Principal Wood, and had never given Dax a thing.

The classwork went on methodically, no matter what was happening to the students and their powers. Dax learned that there was a very simple reason for this.

'It's an anchor,' Mrs Dann told him at the end of one geography lesson.

Everyone knew that Craig Hansen had had a shocking morning when his spirit guide had allowed through a particularly persistent spirit, who kept taking over the poor boy's person. All through maths, Craig had been struggling, and not just with algebra. 'RUM!' he kept shouting, in a thick, mad voice that was absolutely *not* his own and with a face which puckered and sagged like an elderly drunk. In the end they'd had to get Mrs Sartre in to take him down the corridor and help him see off the unwelcome guest.

Dax had been amazed to find Craig, looking pale and shaky, back in the next class.

'The thing is,' Mrs Dann said to Dax, as everyone filed out afterwards. 'If we keep halting things and pulling everything up short whenever there's an incident, it messes up the flow of schoolwork, but it also gives much more weight to anything strange that's happened. And let's be honest, Dax, you and your classmates are going to have to get used to strange things happening on a regular basis. If Craig had spent all afternoon having a lie down, he'd only have dwelt even more upon his experience. Back in here we managed to distract him with the development problems of the Chichester floodplains. And you can see that he's looking much better now.'

It was true. Craig looked perfectly at ease as he left the class, although he wolfed three bars of chocolate at lunch. Tregarren College always kept a good supply of it.

Hallowe'en passed unremarkably, considering their close connection to the spirit world. 'It's all a load of hype,' said Jessica Moorland, tartly, when Dax asked if anything special was going on. True, there were a few hollowed-out pumpkins around, their jaggedly cut mouths and eyes flickering with candlelight, but the college hadn't planned any event around the date. Mr Wood preferred to concentrate on November the Fifth and there was to be a huge bonfire on the edge of the school sports field.

What was also exceptional about bonfire night was that the principal had given permission to the school's illusionists to put on their own firework display. ('They save a fortune,' said Gideon, drily.) They had been rehearsing for weeks with an assortment of illusions. About ten of them, including Spook, met in the dining hall each evening on the run up to the display, secretly practising their glamour and planning their running order. It brought an agreeable air of anticipation to the college and brightened all the students immensely.

The only thing that slightly dampened Dax's spirits was that he hadn't yet managed to become a fox during Development with Owen. He felt fairly confident that he could do it again alone, and was waiting for another full moon so he could get out again, this time with Gideon. He'd promised faithfully that he'd wake his friend next time. But although he tried and tried, he simply couldn't manage to shift in the company of Owen and the ever-present, silently scribbling Mr Eades.

At one point, Dax had leaned in towards Owen, before the start of the hypnosis session, and whispered, 'Look—does *he* have to be here? I might get on better without him.'

'Part 15, subsection A, clause 3.8 of your Tregarren College agreement states,' said Mr Eades, loudly and coldly, 'that no Child Of Limitless Ability shall be developed in the company of fewer than *two* trained witnesses. *TWO.*'

Owen grinned sympathetically at Dax and gave a small shrug.

Dax looked at the mirrored wall and then gave Owen another grin. It was something he'd worked out since that feeling of a *third* person who wasn't there, during his earlier session. The mirror, of course, was two-way. They were being studied. It didn't bother him unduly, but he didn't want Owen to think he was duped. '*Three* witnesses, I reckon.' He mostly mouthed the words this time.

Owen's grin faded. He looked at the mirror and back at Dax. He gave an almost imperceptible nod. 'Clever boy,' he said.

They tried various other exercises and techniques

which were meant to release some of the cold, stored-up anger that Mrs Sartre had been so concerned about. Along with the deep breathing and relaxation, Dax also got to visualize all his worst enemies sitting in an empty chair opposite him, and was encouraged to tell them exactly what he thought of them. It was quite fun, but slightly ridiculous.

He also got the chance to whack a large bean-bag repeatedly with a rounders bat, thinking of those same enemies. He was happy to picture Matthew and Toby and definitely Gina, but he remained cheerful throughout. Apparently he was *supposed* to break down and have a good cry at some point during these sessions. It didn't happen.

'Don't worry,' he'd said to Owen afterwards. 'I never cry. I haven't had a good blub since I was four.'

'That's what worries us,' said Owen. 'You should try it, once in a while. I mean, not all over French class, although with some of the pronunciation that goes on in there, even *I* could weep. But just once in a while, when your throat gets lumpy and your eyes well up—go with it. Let some of it out. You'll feel better.'

But Dax wasn't aware of much cold anger clunking inside him any more, not even when he got a letter from home, from Alice, including a photo of his old bedroom. Gina had really gone to town on it, painting it a lurid violet shade and putting up lacy curtains and a lightshade which looked like a wedding cake on a rope. They were calling it the Dolls' Annexe, and indeed, all

Alice's little pink plastic friends were arranged in neat rows across his bed, which had been covered with a new pink spread. 'But we *will* take the dolls out, when you get home,' promised Alice in her short letter. She didn't ask how Dax was getting on, but he didn't mind. He really didn't want to share any part of his new life with Alice and Gina, although he would have liked to have seen his dad. He'd had only one short postcard from Rob Jones, with an Aberdeen postmark. *'Really pleased to hear you've gone off to be a genius! You obviously got your mother's brains, son,'* he'd written. *'I hope to get down to see you before the end of term. Make me proud. Love, Dad.'*

November the Fifth dawned promisingly crisp and cold, with a clear blue sky and a steady, but not gusty, sea breeze. Dax and Gideon went down to help with the bonfire. As the rules seemed to have been relaxed a little, Gideon sat up on the nearby fence and lifted stick after stick with his mind, placing each one deftly at the high peak of the bonfire-in-waiting while the less able students piled more sticks and branches around the base.

Dax whistled. 'You're getting really good at this.'

Gideon spun a chunky branch of ash around a few times for effect, and then rested it gently on the top. 'It's a gift,' he said, modestly.

'Actually,' he said, jumping down off the fence and walking with Dax back up the field. 'It's not *that* much of a gift. I don't think they're very impressed with me in Development. Christina Tope can lift a TV now. They've started to take her off and give her sessions on her own. I *wish* I could do better. I practise all the time—well, except in Mrs Dann's class, obviously—but I'm still on the baby stuff. Mrs Sartre says I've just got to *mean it more*. What on earth is *that* supposed to mean?'

'Dunno.' Dax shrugged. 'I've got to learn to cry apparently.'

They both spluttered with laughter. 'This'll help,' said Gideon. Spook was walking towards them, followed by some of the other illusionists in dress rehearsal. He strode with style, wearing a long, flowing black cape and black trousers and shirt. He lifted both hands and moved them up in a graceful arc, and a curve of glitter fell in their wake. The glitter was real, but next the air shuddered around him and Gideon murmured, 'Now that *is* quite effective, I must admit.'

'What? What?' said Dax, wishing again that he *could* see glamour.

'He just let off about fifteen jumping squibs,' said Gideon, leaping backwards as if the fireworks really were bouncing about in sparks at his feet. 'Whoa! The others are doing it now.'

To Dax it just looked like a rather dull dance routine, as each of the illusionists raised their arms, copying Spook, and strode on past.

'I wish I could see it,' said Dax. 'It's going to be pretty boring for me tonight.'

'No—it's brilliant, Dax,' said Gideon, earnestly. 'Just follow me and pretend. I wish *I* was a resistant. It's a very rare thing, you know. You haven't told anyone, have you?'

'No—nobody knows except you and Barry,' said Dax, but he remembered the long hard stare from Principal Wood over his coffee cup some days ago, and he wasn't completely sure.

They'd been let off classes, even though it was a Friday, so that everyone could pitch in with the bonfire and so that the illusionists could rehearse and then get some rest before their performance. Dax and Gideon hung around the joint common room and, to his surprise, Dax saw Lisa Hardman approaching him again. She walked towards him and then jerked her head in the direction of the door. It was the first communication she'd had with him since their woodsman group had made the leaf hut. Over the past few days, if anything, she seemed to have become even *more* withdrawn. Curious, Dax followed the girl outside and she led him to a quiet corner behind the dorms.

'I have another message,' she said dully.

She looked worn out, thought Dax. Clearly the midnight running sessions weren't working as well as she'd hoped.

'Look, Lisa, when I spoke to Owen, he said that you could come and talk to him any time, and that he was sure he could help you,' said Dax.

Lisa glared at him. 'You didn't tell him it was *me* did you?' she demanded.

'No! No, of course not. But he probably guessed. I mean, you *are* the only COLA who refuses point blank to go into Development, aren't you?' This Dax had heard, around the college.

183

Lisa looked at her feet and then shrugged. 'It doesn't matter,' she said. 'I'm not going to see him. But it would give me a bit of a break, if you could just pass this one on. Could you?'

Dax shrugged at her stubbornness and then nodded.

'OK.' Lisa took a deep breath, as if she was limbering up to throw a punch. 'The name is Georgia Felstein—Georgia Felstein. And she's a very persistent lady,' she added, wearily. 'She says it's *not* Michael. He didn't do it. They need to find the sailor. Please, Dax, tell them to find the sailor . . .' her voice tailed off into unutterable weariness.

'What does it mean?' asked Dax, fascinated.

'*I* don't know. He probably cracked her on the head with a bottle of rum or something. She's dead, isn't she? And she's got a voice that could cut glass, so please, please, pass it on. At least there might be something good to come out of it this time, if someone's been accused of something they didn't do. It would be nice to think there's *some* point to all this.'

She walked away without looking back. 'You're welcome!' Dax shouted after her, sarcastically. Suffering spirit abuse or not, that girl was such a brat, he thought.

The fireworks display was a big hit. From the very start Spook and his fellow illusionists had the audience entranced. Literally. Except for Dax, of course. Dax *did* find that when he concentrated very hard, and leaned with his elbows on both Gideon's and Barry's shoulders, sitting up on the fence behind them, he occasionally got a faint idea of what everyone else was seeing and hearing.

The mass hypnosis was so strong that some of it leached into him and he saw a couple of particularly splendid showers of green and silver fire high in the sky and heard their crash bounce back off the calm sea. He enjoyed the atmosphere and the crackling heat of the bonfire, and made sure he looked where Barry and Gideon looked and made the same noises of delight and wonder. He was extremely pleased when he found that the sparklers that were getting handed round were *real*.

Down on a small platform some distance from the giant, blazing bonfire, Spook was in his element. He strutted confidently and conducted the whole display, with back-up from his team, as if he were leading the Royal Philharmonic Orchestra. At the final burst of applause and cheering, he bowed with a flourish and led the team back up through the crowd in a storm of clapping. Passing by Dax, he couldn't resist saying, 'Impressive enough for you, fox-boy?'

'I have to say,' said Dax, 'I've never seen anything like it.'

Gideon and Barry snorted behind him and Spook's triumphant grin wavered a little before he marched on. The boys collapsed into fits of giggles, and then Dax realized they were being watched. Principal Wood was following the performers and he was looking searchingly, despite the proud smile on his face, at Dax. Dax pulled himself together quickly and eased back into the crowd.

'Come on,' he said to the others. 'Let's go and get a hotdog.'

The school dining hall had opened its wide glass doors and was sending out delicious wafts of frying onions, sausages, and hot tomato soup. Everyone began to troop up the steps towards it, rubbing their hands together in the November night air.

Barry, Dax, and Gideon collected the mugs of steaming orange soup in one hand and a napkin-wrapped hotdog in the other and ambled back across the dining room to look for somewhere to sit.

'It *was* good,' said Gideon. 'Even if it was Spook's show. Although there's no way he could have done all those rockets without a load of other people working with him. On his own it would have been one dodgy Catherine wheel whacking backwards and forwards and going pop.'

'Did you see the train, though?' said Barry, taking a mouthful of hotdog and depositing a large blob of ketchup on the end of his nose, which was whistling with appreciation. 'The train was brilliant. They made it go right across the sky,' he added, for Dax's benefit.

'Enjoy the fireworks, did you, boys?' said a charming voice behind them and Dax jumped. They turned round to see Principal Wood, holding a mug of soup and beaming at them good-naturedly. Gideon and Barry talked enthusiastically about the display.

Dax smiled and nodded and tried very hard to be part of it. 'I loved that green and silver one,' he ventured, anxiously.

'And what did you think of the finale, Dax?' said the principal, smiling warmly at him and never moving his eyes from Dax's. Dax floundered. He hadn't even the *faintest* idea what the finale had been. He could make a wild guess about the train, but he could be wrong. 'It was—it was amazing,' he said.

'But could you make out what it was meant to *be*?' prodded Mr Wood and Dax felt him push at his mind again. Not to try to fog him with glamour now, but to uncover Dax's own defences.

'You said you thought it was a dog, Dax,' prompted Gideon, off to his right. Dax blinked.

'Yes . . . it did look a bit like one,' he hedged, feeling panicky.

'Not a dog, Dax,' the principal gave him a friendly punch on the shoulder. 'A fox! A fox! In honour of our first and probably our last shapeshifter!' His voice was jovial but his eyes glittered and for the first time Dax decided, completely, that he *didn't* trust Patrick Wood. Not at *all*.

'Phew, that was close,' chuckled Gideon as the principal, thankfully, moved on. 'I think we covered for you though.'

But Dax wasn't paying attention. Over Gideon's shoulder he could see Lisa, standing motionless in a sea of students. She was holding a tray of china mugs filled with hot soup and she was looking very hard at Principal Wood, who was now chatting to Spook. As he watched, Dax saw the colour drain from the girl's face, and she moved her dark eyes from Mr Wood, across to Dax, and then back again. Then her tray of mugs crashed to the floor.

18

As the dining room ladies fussed around her with wet cloths and dustpans, Lisa slowly picked up the broken china, helped by one or two other students. She seemed dazed and didn't speak. When she got up to go, some moments later, she was quite unaware of the splashes of tomato soup across her expensive pale cream jacket. There was even some on her cheek, which she made no effort to wipe away as she walked past Dax and Barry and Gideon. The lively chatter had resumed across the dining hall, but Dax was concerned. And not just for Lisa.

Something had been bothering him about Mia for some days now, too, and he couldn't work out exactly what, but as Lisa pushed through the double doors to the path that led back up to the dorms, her face still pale and closed, Mia was coming through the other way. Lisa shoved into her, unwittingly, but only gave the vaguest of nods of apology before disappearing into the night. Mia immediately smiled her forgiveness, as Mia always did, but Dax noticed that her hand was shaking as she lifted it to push some hair off her face. There were shadows under her eyes and she walked slowly, as if she were sixty years older.

'Hi, Mia.' Dax walked across to her and then shuffled,

awkwardly. He wanted to give her an arm, to help and steady her, but it didn't seem like the kind of thing you did with a twelve-year-old girl.

'Dax.' She smiled her wonderful, warm smile, and he felt that familiar wave of attachment that they all felt. 'I hear you're getting on well.' *Nothing* stayed secret for long around here, thought Dax, uneasily.

'Yes—well—I'm getting used to being the weird shapeshifty type,' he said. 'How is it going for you? Do they bring people in for you to heal?'

Mia laughed and shook her head. 'No—it's a lot of group work. Channelling energies together and things like that. We can't go out and kick someone on the shin every five minutes so we can practise making it all better. But I usually do a few people across the week, when they need it.'

'I don't know why they bother with the sanatorium, then,' said Dax, but he wondered how often Mia was called upon to heal her classmates, and remembered Owen refusing to let her heal him up in the wood. Maybe that was just a teacher thing, Dax thought. Maybe there were technically meant to be two trained witnesses present for everyone else, too. The college tried hard to make the most bizarre happenings comply to red tape. Even the spirit messages had to be checked and signed by Mr Eades on the little pink Spirit Communication Notice slips before they could be delivered.

'Have you seen Mr Hind?' asked Mia, scanning the busy room.

'No—I think he might be down by the bonfire still,' said Dax.

Mia glanced down the stone steps and along to the dark figures silhouetted around the reddening glow of the bonfire, which was slowly sinking into itself and turning to embers. She considered for a moment, and then shook her head and said, 'No—I'll wait to see him in the morning. I need to go to bed now.' And with what seemed like immense concentration, Mia turned and walked slowly back to the double doors. 'Night, Dax,' she called over her shoulder.

As they clambered into bed, everyone later than usual, with their hair smelling of smoke, Dax pulled the covers over his head and tried to block out the growing feeling of unease that was plaguing him. Mr Wood, Lisa, Mia . . . the wolf. He didn't understand why he was feeling so troubled, but he wished the feeling would leave him alone. He felt a glimmer of sympathy for Lisa and wished, again, that she would go to Owen.

Owen had made no pretence when Dax had delivered him the second message. 'For pity's sake, Dax. Tell her that she *has* to come and see me. Or Mrs Sartre; it doesn't matter who. She needs to learn how to deal with this stuff.'

Dax had shrugged. 'I'll tell her,' he said.

Owen had patted him on the shoulder. 'It's something that she's got you, anyway,' he'd said.

For what it's worth, thought Dax, as he fell asleep.

* * *

Everything seemed brighter in the morning. It was another sunny day, although an overnight frost had iced the grass around the dorms and given a soft, silvery coating to the roofs. It was a Saturday when Gideon and Dax could go into Polgammon, and late in the morning, after a lie in to recover from the bonfire party, they headed up to the tower gate with their allowance money in their pockets. Gideon planned that they'd have a walk through the wood which skirted the marshes, the long way round to the village, and then get a fish-and-chips lunch. He was badly hoping that Dax would change into a fox once they got to the wood.

'Think about it,' he said. 'If you can get to be a fox just by imagining you're lying on the floor of the wood, you should be able to do it easily when you actually *are*!'

Dax agreed that it was definitely worth a try and once outside they split off from the other students wandering down the direct road to the village and ran up into the wood.

The problem was, thought Dax, the ground was so much more comfortable in his imagination than it was in reality. He wriggled and reached under his back to haul out a sharp chunk of rock which had been lying just beneath the leaf litter, and chucked it off into the undergrowth. Gideon sat in the branches of a nearby tree, looking down at him excitedly. 'Go on!' he said. 'Go on! Hurry up! Relax!' Dax laughed. How on earth could he relax with Gideon jiggling up and down in an oak, nearly bursting with anticipation?

'I don't think it's going to work,' he said. 'And my bum's getting wet.'

'*Con*centrate!' ordered Gideon. 'Look—I'll be quiet! I won't say a word for five minutes! Shhh! Go on!'

Dax tried very hard, and after maybe three minutes or so he did succeed in slowing down his breathing a little. Then a late bee flew into his ear and he was up on his feet, shaking his head and yelling and smacking his hair in a frenzy.

Gideon wailed with disappointment. 'If I didn't know better I'd think you were making the whole thing up!' he grumbled, sliding back down out of the tree.

Dax was fed up. 'Thanks a bunch.' he said. He really wanted to show Gideon. He would have loved to be able to shift easily, at will, whenever he wanted. Maybe he would be able to one day, but at the moment it was just not happening.

He stomped off into the wood and Gideon followed a few yards behind, kicking leaves and not offering any words of comfort. It was the first time they'd really fallen out and Dax felt a little cloud of gloom descend over him. It wasn't fair. Everyone else seemed to be able to do amazing things with just a hard stare or a flick of their little finger. Why did *he* have to work so hard? Dax felt the merest, familiar bubble of the old angry lava again and immediately squashed it back down. Stop being so pathetic, he told himself. Think of Lisa. You want to watch what you wish for, boy.

A small silver square dropped lightly onto his head

and slid down his nose. Laughing, Dax caught the chunk of chocolate; Gideon's trademark. He turned and waited for his friend to catch up.

'Sorry,' said Gideon. 'I know it's hard for you. But you'll do it soon. I know you will.'

They walked on in companionable silence, munching chocolate. The snap of dead twigs and the resonant thud of the ground beneath their feet felt good. Dax could smell the dog-fox nearby, probably curled up in its hole under a log, and he smiled to himself. At the edge of the wood, near the marsh, a green woodpecker flashed up out of the low bushes with a startled *kee-kee-kee* and alighted a safe distance away on an ash tree, before beginning a little drumming. In the distance the sea sighed and breathed and sighed and breathed.

The marsh looked very solid today, with the hard frost still clinging to the ground. Gideon led Dax out on to the gravel path that wound across it. 'We go across, over the bridge and round that little hill, and it joins up to the road that goes back into the village from another direction,' he said. They trooped along the path and paused on the wooden bridge to gaze in awe at the bright green stuff that snaked beneath it.

'It just looks like moss or lichen or something,' said Dax, stretching his foot out under the guard rail of the little bridge. He put his toe on to the surface and it felt quite firm. 'See?' he said to Gideon.

Gideon grinned and said, 'Push a little harder.'

Dax drove his shoe down harder and there was a

small sigh of escaping gas and the green stuff around his foot broke apart in little crazed chunks, revealing a dark brown slime under the surface. It made a sucking noise and held on for a second as Dax pulled back his foot in shock, and Gideon laughed.

'See?' he said. 'Still want to walk across it?'

'No thanks,' said Dax. He watched as the green stuff drifted back over the slime, like a rapidly healing wound.

'Come on,' said Gideon. 'I'm starved.'

They walked on across the marsh path, past the notices warning dog walkers to keep their pets on a leash and stick to the marked walkway, and up the hill. Joining the road on the other side, they hiked round the base of the hill and down into the village in time for lunch. They could smell the promise of their fish-and-chips five minutes before they sat down at the red-checked cafe table.

'The best fish-and-chips in England,' said Gideon, with fervour. 'The fish comes in to Penzance first thing in the morning and arrives here in a little box of ice, while the last poor haddock is still flapping and gasping. It doesn't get better than that! They don't die in vain,' he added, his mouth full of fish and batter.

Dax laughed. 'You'd better not say that to the healers. They're nearly all vegetarians.'

'Huh!' snorted Gideon, emptying a red slick of ketchup across his chips. 'They'd live on thin air if someone told them carrots could feel a fork. Lord help them if they ever had to fend for themselves.'

The meal was everything that Gideon had promised, delivered by a cheerful, plump young Cornishwoman in a striped pinafore who came over to offer a top up of chips. Gideon waved her away with a grin. 'Thanks, Mrs Wilson, but I need to leave a bit of space.'

She poked him in the shoulder in a friendly way. 'I know where *you're* off to next. I don't know where you put it, Gideon!' Gideon beamed and wiped his mouth with the red checked napkin before swiftly draining the last of his lemonade. He checked his watch.

'I'm just going to nip across to the Chocolate Parlour before all the almond crunch is gone,' he said. 'Can you pay up here and I'll give you my half when I've got some change?' Dax nodded, still working his way through the huge portion of haddock.

'I'll catch you up,' he said, knowing how Gideon loved to linger in the Chocolate Parlour, taking his time over choosing the next fortnight's rations. Dax finished his meal without hurrying, enjoying the sights and smells and sounds around him. The small cafe was packed with occupied tables and customers had to squeeze past most of them sideways to find a seat. A fat fryer was permanently bubbling in the open kitchen and hissed angrily every time fresh potato or battered fish was lowered into it. People were chatting contentedly and the cutlery continually chinked as twenty or so diners foraged across their plates.

Finishing, Dax eased back in his chair with a satisfied sigh. He would be very happy to do this every fortnight, he decided, reaching into his coat pocket for his COLA allowance money. He dug in deeper, his fingers not meeting the crisp fold of paper he was seeking. Concerned, Dax sat up and rifled more thoroughly through his pockets, depositing their entire contents on the table in front of him. Where was his money? Blast! He realized that it must have fallen out when he was lying on the wood floor, failing to turn into a fox.

'All right, my love?' Mrs Wilson called across from the counter.

Dax blushed furiously. 'I'm sorry . . . I . . . I seem to have lost my money.'

Mrs Wilson folded her vinegary arms and gave him a sceptical look. Dax realized she must have heard this before. Only it was *true*. 'Can I just catch up with my friend . . . ?' he began, desperately, when a cool voice cut across him.

'It's OK,' said the blonde woman, opening her purse and handing Mrs Wilson a note. 'I'll pay for Dax and his friend.'

Dax sank back into his chair in a wave of horror. It was Caroline Fisher.

19

She was neatly dressed in a well-cut, tweedy trouser suit and had on some high-heeled brown leather boots which matched her bag. Sitting down opposite Dax, Caroline Fisher smiled at him and gave a knowing little wink.

'How have you been, Dax?' she said, as if they were on the best of terms.

He was speechless. He stared at her, wondering what on earth to do. She collected the empty plates and glasses and deposited them all on the vacant table next to them, dusted some batter crumbs off the checked tablecloth with Dax's napkin, and then rested her elbows on the table, tucking her short blonde hair behind her ears and regarding Dax with a winning smile.

'It's taken me ages to find you,' she said. 'But I knew I'd track you down in the end. It's just too good a story, Dax,' she added, shaking her head and spreading her hands as if in apology.

'What?' spluttered Dax, angrily but as quietly as he could. 'Catching the Beast of Bark's End?'

'Oh, so you've seen that?' She chuckled and then had the grace to look a little sheepish. 'Yes, well, that was a *bit* over the top, I grant you. But I was feeling inspired. It's been a long time since we had anything more scary than a wheel clamper in Bark's End. You can't really blame me.'

'Oh yes I can,' hissed Dax. 'And if you think I'm going to talk to you, you've got another think coming!'

He got up to go but she rested her long-fingered hand on his arm and said in a warning kind of voice, 'Dax, sit down. You don't want to get caught up in a scene, do you?'

He stared at her, wondering what she would do. What she *could* do. 'I could lose control, you know,' she told him, in answer to his thoughts. 'I could start screaming, because, after all, I'm just a girl and I'm sure I recognize you as the boy who went wild and savaged two children. It's really terribly frightening.'

Looking around him in horror, hoping nobody had heard, Dax sank unsteadily back into his seat. His brain was doing back-flips, trying to find a quick way out of this situation. How much did she know—or more to the point, how much did she *believe*?

'Look,' he said, attempting a thin little laugh, 'surely you can't believe all that wild animal stuff. I mean—it's ridiculous, isn't it?'

'Well, you know,' she said, leaning across the table towards him and speaking conspiratorially. 'That's what *I* thought at first. I mean, I thought *something* had certainly happened in that basement. There's no smoke without fire. But I thought it was more likely to be about some young lads having a crack at the caretaker's whisky, and things getting out of control. That's what I thought at first.

'And to be honest, even when I spoke to Matthew

and later to his parents, I still thought it could be that. I mean, he's hardly the brightest match in the box, is he? And Toby looked like one big attention seeker. People *like* to get press attention sometimes, especially if they think they might get some money out of a school, in compensation.

'In fact, it was meeting *you* that changed my mind. There was something about the way you reacted which made me think. Made me do a bit more digging. And then your friend Clive, too, bless him. Decent little chap—terrible clothes. He was *so* protective of you. Wouldn't say a *word.* Wouldn't even confirm your age. So anyway, to cut a long story short, I happened to be looking through the websites of a few of our sister papers and rival rags up and down the country, and blow me down, if there aren't a *load* of reports over the last few months of children allegedly doing really bizarre things. Like floating bits of cutlery in the air, or touching a friend and healing their sprained wrist; vanishing into thin air, or suddenly upping and giving over messages from the dead.

'And you know what else? *All* of these kids are about the same age. And, from what I can tell, they all vanish out of the community in a matter of weeks, or even days, after the public witnesses what they're doing. Now, where, I thought, *where* have they all gone? And where did Dax Jones go? Of course, I spoke to your mum—only she's your stepmum, isn't she? Because there aren't any real mums left, are there?' Dax shivered at her accuracy.

'And she tells me that you're a genius and off to genius school. Looks pretty happy about it, too.' Dax nodded wryly, in spite of himself.

'Dax, look,' said Caroline, touching his arm and adopting a very reasonable tone. 'I didn't come down here because I want to stitch you up, and I'm sorry about all that Beast of Bark's End nonsense, but I've been making a few discreet enquiries around here and I know that there's some pretty amazing stuff happening over that hill at the college. Of course the locals are pretty tight-lipped about it and they keep insisting it's just a unit of academic excellence, but one or two of them opened up about some things they'd heard. And, Dax, come *on*! I checked out your school results up until last term.' She held up her hands and shrugged as he glared at her. 'Look, it's all down the local education authority offices; it's quite legal. And it's clear that you're a bright boy, but you're no genius. We both know that.'

Dax looked at her levelly. She gazed back with her wide grey eyes and spoke softly. 'I just think, if we have something extraordinary happening among our children, the public deserves to know,' she said. 'And don't you think it's all a bit sinister, whisking you all off down the end of the country and hiding you behind a pile of granite? How do you know that it's for your own good? How do you know that it's not just a way of stopping you doing anything that the government doesn't want? Eh?'

This had never occurred to Dax before. He didn't want it to occur to him now. He stood up with resolve and headed for the cafe door. Caroline Fisher sighed, rose, and followed him outside.

'I'm not going to drop this, Dax,' she warned as she tailed him up the cobbled street, buttoning up her jacket in the chilly November air. 'Perhaps you should tell your teacher about me. Perhaps you should give a message to the headmaster.'

'Principal,' corrected Dax, testily.

'Principal, then,' she agreed. She took hold of his arm and pulled him into a doorway. 'Tell your principal that if he agrees to an interview, I will allow him copy approval. That means he'll get to check everything before it's printed.'

'I know what it means,' growled Dax.

'If he doesn't agree,' she said, 'then I'll get the story my own way. And the first he'll know about it is when the world's press starts camping out on Tregarren College's doorstep. Have you got that?' she checked, looking hard into his face. Dax wanted to hit her. He felt absolutely cornered.

'I'll tell him,' he muttered. Caroline Fisher smiled, briefly, and then dug out a card with her name and mobile phone number printed on it, and scribbled details of the hotel she was staying at on the back.

'Give him this. And, Dax,' she said as he shoved it into his pocket and began to move away, 'please don't think I'm the enemy. I could be your saviour.'

'Fishes' pants! What happened to *you*?' said Gideon, as

Dax wandered, dazed, into the Chocolate Parlour. Gideon was just lifting a large bag of goodies off the counter and tucking it under his arm.

Dax stared at him, opened his mouth to speak, and then let it fall shut again. He was shaking and feeling light-headed. Of all the things he'd seen and experienced in the past few weeks, it was one small woman with a notebook that had scared him the most. The thought of bringing such chaos and trouble to COLA Club was appalling to him and he just didn't know what to do. If only he had never laid eyes on her! If only he hadn't told her that he was going away. Idiot! *Idiot!* He was going to ruin it for everyone.

Gideon's curious look gave way to one of concern. 'Come on,' he said, urgently. 'We need to get you back.' He propelled Dax out of the shop door and up the street, back towards the college. 'Tell me what's happened,' he said, when they were some way up the hill and not close to any other students.

'Caroline Fisher has come to hunt down the Beast of Bark's End,' Dax gulped. 'Only she doesn't just want me. She's after all of us.'

They went to Owen first. Gideon knocked hard on the door of his cliff-face cottage and pushed Dax firmly inside, the second Owen opened it. Owen stood back in surprise. 'And to what do I owe the pleasure?' he said, addressing Gideon as Dax sank dispiritedly on to the leather chair by his fire.

'We have a problem,' said Gideon. 'A big problem. Dax's reporter is in Polgammon.'

Owen took a sharp breath and then wandered across to the fireplace, leaning his palms against the narrow brick mantel and resting his forehead against the rough chimney breast above it. 'Sit down, Gideon,' he said, his eyes closed. Gideon sat down on the other chair and then Owen turned and sank, cross-legged, on to the red rug between them, cupping his chin in one hand and regarding Dax seriously. 'Tell me everything. And tell me now,' he said. And his manner reminded Dax of the second day he'd known Owen and their ruthless encounter in the lorry.

Dax related his meeting with Caroline Fisher in detail, ending with the warning she'd given, that if the principal wouldn't allow her an interview she'd do the story anyway and bring the world's press to their door. At this, he handed Owen her card which the man took and read in silence, flipping it over in his fingers. For a long time he said nothing, considering. Then he rose purposefully to his feet and walked through the brick archway and deeper into the cave end of his home.

Dax and Gideon looked at each other, then at the archway. They didn't speak until Owen returned two minutes later, with a mug in each hand. He handed one to each of the boys. 'Blue one for Dax,' he said. 'Extra sugar.' They drank the strong, sweet tea quickly, as Owen shrugged on his warm outdoor coat and put the reporter's card in the pocket.

'Come on, Dax,' he said, at length. 'We need to see Principal Wood.'

He sent Gideon back to the dorm with instructions to talk to nobody about what he knew, and then he and Dax made their way down the winding stone steps and paths towards the main college building, and Patrick Wood's office. Dax was somewhat revived by the sweet tea, but he did not feel good about facing the principal. He could not shake off the deep mistrust he had arrived at last night at the bonfire party and he didn't know if, in his present state, he could hide this.

'Come,' said Mr Wood, when they knocked on the door. He was working through a pile of papers on his desk and he removed his reading glasses and looked up curiously as they entered, before registering almost immediately that something was wrong.

'Dax has had a run-in with a reporter in Polgammon,' said Owen, getting straight to the point. The principal bit one end of the arm of his glasses thoughtfully, but without alarm, peering at Owen and nodding for him to go on. 'This is worse than it sounds,' sighed Owen, sitting on the edge of the principal's desk. 'Pat, I think we need to take this up a level.'

But the principal put down his glasses and leaned back in his chair, tapping his fingers on his desk and pursing his lips thoughtfully. 'No,' he said slowly. 'I'm sure it can be contained, without bothering the department.' He looked at Dax, and Dax noticed that he made no attempt, for the first time, to charm him. 'Tell me everything, Dax.' But here—just a glimmer: 'Don't be afraid. It's not your fault.'

Dax related the whole story again, feeling un-utterably weary. He wanted nothing more than to crawl into his bed under the slanting window and drop down into dreamless sleep. When he'd finished the story, Owen picked up the receiver of the telephone on the principal's desk and handed it to Patrick Wood. 'Pat, we really must,' he urged again. 'This is more than we can deal with.'

But the principal narrowed his eyes at Owen, taking the receiver and holding out his other hand. 'The card please, Owen,' he said, coolly. Owen paused, but then picked out the card and handed it over, and the principal carefully dialled the number on it.

To Dax's astonishment, Mr Wood spoke warmly into the mouthpiece. 'Hello? Is that Miss Fisher? This is Patrick Wood, from Tregarren College. I believe you met one of my students today.' He paused as she responded. 'Yes, yes that's right. Dax Jones. He tells me you are intent on writing a feature about us. Is that so?' Dax could just make out Caroline Fisher's bright, professional tone at the other end of the line.

'Well, I really think you *should* come and meet me, as a matter of fact, Miss Fisher. Yes. Yes, that's what I said. Around one o'clock tomorrow would suit me. In fact, why don't you come for lunch?' Dax couldn't believe his ears. He'd be asking her to stay for a week, next! 'I'd be very happy to show you around,' Mr Wood was saying.

'Absolutely. Not at all. I'll look forward to it. I'll see you tomorrow. Goodbye.'

He replaced the receiver with a gentle click and smiled at Dax and Owen. 'You see. Simple.'

'But what will you tell her?' burst out Dax. 'How will you stop her telling everyone?'

'Dax, I have met more than one journalist in my time,' said Mr Wood. 'I know how they operate. She isn't the threat you think she is. By the time she leaves tomorrow, the sting will have been very firmly removed from her tail. You really don't have to worry.'

But, as they got up to go, Dax realized he'd never felt more worried in his life.

20

He slept badly. He dreamed of the dark shape. The dark shape that had first slunk into his head, sad and hurt, weeks ago, before any of this had ever started. And again he felt no fear of it—it seemed to want to explain something to him. And this time it came closer and in his dream he heard it panting a little.

He felt his mattress dip sharply as it rested its shaggy dark paws on the edge, and sensed its warm breath on his cheek. It could have sunk its teeth into his face at any moment, but it just breathed softly against his half closed eyes and then was gone.

Dax felt deserted. In his dream he called out for it to come back . . . but then he was again in the hot shed with his head stuck in the gap at the back, only he *hadn't* changed into a fox and the whole thing *was* a dream. He had never even gone to COLA Club and Owen and Gideon, Lisa, Mia, and the whole place did not exist.

Gideon shook him awake. 'Dax! Dax! Wake *up*!'

Dax sprang upright and looked around him. He actually pushed Gideon's shoulder to check he was real. And then he sighed and lay back down in his bed, awash with relief.

'You were shouting out in your sleep,' said Gideon,

getting back into his own bed. It was morning, but still early. Barry was wound up in his quilt, snoring gently, with the occasional whistle. 'You were going "No! No! No!" It was *not* a nice way to wake up!'

'Sorry,' mumbled Dax, from his pillow.

'Were you dreaming about *her*? The reporter woman?'

Dax shook his head. He found he couldn't speak about his dream. The terrible desolation he had felt in his sleep was still within his grasp—and now that Gideon had reminded him, a new desolation hit him, which he knew he couldn't wake up from. Caroline Fisher was coming today, and this could spell the end of COLA Club.

'Maybe if you just *talked* to her; maybe you could stop her. Girls like you, Dax. You could charm her a bit.'

Dax shot Gideon a scornful look. 'Girls do *not* like me,' he said. 'Well, no more than anyone else. And I don't *do* charm.'

'Lisa Hardman likes you,' said Gideon, with a teasing note to his voice. 'I've seen her looking at you.'

'Yeah, but that's . . . ' Dax shut his mouth, before he gave away another secret which wasn't his to give. 'That's because she's short-sighted and too vain to wear her glasses,' he improvised.

The morning dragged terribly. Being a Sunday, there were no classes, although if you practised a faith there were meetings and singing and so on in the quiet meditation area at the far end of the college building. Dax did not practise a faith. He realized, glumly, as he and Gideon mooched across the sports field towards the sea, that he hadn't really had faith in anything for the past seven years. Not until he met Owen and came to COLA Club.

He and Gideon climbed over the fence and made their way along a short cut to the rocks around the lido. The sounds of the becalmed, captured sea, lapping gently in its shallow basin of rocks, and the birds that coasted through the air above it, were comforting. They wandered up and down, poking into rock pools and frightening crabs. Dax glanced at his watch. 11.53. She'd be here in not much more than an hour. He'd never be able to get any lunch down. He felt sick with dread.

He badly needed some reassurance and so he left Gideon at the lido, and wandered unhappily back up the cliff paths in hopes of finding Owen. Dax had just lifted his fist to knock on the door of the cob cottage when his fox sense suddenly opened up and his hearing sharpened acutely. Owen was talking to someone inside and by her accent, Dax realized it was Paulina Sartre.

' . . . can't carry this alone,' Owen was saying. 'It worries me. I think he's dangerous. Why not call in Chambers?'

'Because Tregarren means everything to him,' replied Paulina Sartre, and there was a low note of anxiety in her voice.

There was a pause, during which Owen exhaled loudly. 'It means everything to me too. There's not much I wouldn't do to protect it.'

'But, Owen,' said Paulina Sartre, slowly and carefully. 'Who do we protect it *from*?'

Dax suddenly realized that she was moving towards the door and he was standing there, gaping, his fist still frozen in the air. In a split second he had bounded away down the path, and as she emerged from the cottage doubled back as if he were just bounding *up* for the first time.

Paulina Sartre smiled at him. 'Good morning, Dax,' she said, without any trace of the concern she had been radiating behind Owen's door. 'Are you quite well?'

Dax paused three steps below her and looked at her appraisingly. She was an empath, wasn't she?

'Ah, I see you are not,' she said, still smiling. 'It is to be expected. Try not to worry; I am sure Mr Wood will sort things out.' She went to pass him on the steps but suddenly stopped beside him and said quietly, 'If you are thinking of going to see someone, Dax, be sure it is Mr Hind . . . or me. Please don't trouble the principal today.'

It wasn't her words that sent a chill through him as she walked gracefully on down the steps. It was the unmistakable scent. He now realized the pulse of fear he'd smelt in the principal's study when they'd all first met undoubtedly came from Paulina Sartre. Did she think he was dangerous, too?

He heard Owen's door shut and decided not to see him. From what he'd just heard, Owen was probably not in the mood for the boy who'd brought such a threat to his beloved Tregarren College. Dax felt another wave of shame and dread. It would probably have been better if Owen had never found him.

In the event, lunch was far worse than he could possibly have imagined. He went into the dining room with Gideon, not because he was remotely interested in food, but because he needed the company of his friend and the other students around him. He picked up a roll and some chicken soup and joined Gideon at a table with Mia and Barry. He didn't say much as they all chatted on about the bonfire night and what their plans were for Christmas; whether they were going home or not.

Dax felt that their contented lives were made of spun sugar and, thanks to him, were about to be crunched into tiny pieces at any time. Once the whole world knew about this place, people would come pouring down, trying to see what was happening. They'd camp out in the wood at the top of the cliff with binoculars and cameras and clog up the narrow road outside, queueing to get in and begging to get messages from their dead relatives, to see kids moving stuff with their minds, to be healed . . .

This last thought made him glance at Mia. She didn't look as bad as she had on Bonfire Night, but he noticed that her hands were still shaking a little, and that dark shadows still marked a tired curve under each of her eyes. He wondered what was happening with Mia, and resolved to ask her, straight out, when he got a chance.

He was unable to swallow one mouthful of his soup, and simply sat, stirring it and gazing at the table. Then Gideon breathed 'Oh, boy,' and nudged him.

Dax looked up and saw, to his horror, that Principal Wood was entering the dining hall, *with* Caroline Fisher. She was dressed in another well-cut trouser suit and peering round in great excitement, her shining, wide eyes devouring the room full of students she had worked so hard to see. The principal was charming her thoroughly, Dax noticed. He touched the small of her back lightly, and then her shoulder, guiding her across to the canteen area and collecting a tray for her. He smiled and continually sought eye contact, occasionally running his hands through his boyish mop of brown hair in a disarming gesture.

Dax felt a small stirring of hope. Maybe if Mr Wood worked really hard on her, she'd fall for his charm so much that she would be persuaded to go home and leave them all alone. She was certainly enjoying herself; laughing and smiling back at him and touching her own hair a lot as if she was his mirror image. Dax froze as they turned, with laden trays, and the principal pointed across the room. She raised a pretty eyebrow and nodded, with another self-satisfied smile, and they both headed across to join Dax and his table.

He felt Gideon tense up alongside him as the pair settled themselves in two empty seats between Dax and Mia. 'Good morning, students,' said Mr Wood, warmly. 'I'd like you to meet Miss Fisher. She's come here today to find out about Tregarren College and the COLA Club.'

Caroline Fisher said 'Hi!' brightly to them all as he introduced them by name.

'And Dax, of course,' said the principal, 'you already know.'

She smiled at him and looked hard into his eyes. 'Good to see you again, Dax,' she said. To her credit, she did manage to keep the triumph out of her voice. Dax didn't answer her, but went back to stirring his soup.

'I've been telling Miss Fisher about what we do here and why it's so important, at this stage, to keep you all protected from the general public, until we're all a little older and wiser,' went on the principal, and the charm and appeal of his manner washed over them all. Except Dax.

Although he could sense the charm, it seemed, as usual, to run around him in a stream, rather than flow across him. The others felt it, though, and as usual they were giving the principal their rapt attention, as was Caroline Fisher. She even reached across and picked a stray breadcrumb off his lapel at one point, and he smiled broadly back at her and brushed his hand across his jacket to remove any others that might be there. It *was* working, Dax had to hand it to the man. She was utterly, utterly charmed. He felt a little unwilling admiration for Patrick Wood. He had seemed very confident that he could handle the situation and maybe Dax and Owen *should* have trusted him more. Maybe.

After lunch the principal took Caroline off for a tour of the college. They could see him, at a distance, walking her around the quad, then across to the dormitories, where she was introduced to more bemused students, then down to the sports field and around the top end of the lido. The sun was warm, for a November day, and the sea wind not too strong. Caroline Fisher strode along in her high heeled leather boots, her blonde bob waving in the gentle breeze, saturated in the principal's best quality charm and completely unaware of it. By the time they headed back up the little stone steps towards the gatehouse, some two hours later, she had her arm tucked into Mr Wood's as if they were a couple. But if he thought that the principal would settle for this, Dax was mistaken.

One of the psychics ran across to Gideon and Dax. 'Mr Wood needs you, Gideon,' he panted. He handed Gideon an envelope and the boy ripped it open quickly and extracted a slip of white paper. He showed it to Dax as he read it.

Written in the principal's high, neat letters was the message: 'Gideon, meet us at the gate tower NOW and use your powers to remove and hide a small tape recorder which is in Miss Fisher's bag. It's an open-topped basket so it shouldn't be a problem. Be *careful* and be quick.' He had initialled it. Gideon showed the note to Dax and they set off, running, up the steps to the gate tower.

At almost halfway up, Dax was suddenly hailed, urgently. He looked over his shoulder, ready to wave off any interference. He *must* get to the tower with Gideon and find out if everything was going to be all right. Ahead of him, the principal and Caroline Fisher were pushing open the gate tower door.

'Dax! I've got to talk to you! *Now!*' It was Lisa, racing up the steps after him, looking flushed and agitated.

'Sorry, Lisa,' Dax called down. 'You'll have to give me a message a bit later. I really can't stop.'

'Dax, you *have* to,' yelled Lisa, still chasing him frantically. 'You *have* to! It's about *you!*'

Dax paused on the steps, exasperated. Gideon ran on up. 'I'll catch you up, in about ten seconds,' he called after him, turning to Lisa with some annoyance. 'Look, Lisa, I appreciate it, but whatever it is, it has to be quick. I need to be up in that tower.'

'No, Dax, you don't,' she said, and her face was tense with warning. She took hold of his arm. 'I can feel you falling,' she said, and there was a shake in her voice. 'I've been getting it from that dratted animal since Bonfire Night. It's not good, Dax, it's really not good.'

Dax stared at her, feeling confused and alarmed. 'But what difference does it make?' he blurted out, coldly. 'You said yourself, it doesn't make any difference what you say or do. If I'm going to fall, I'm going to fall. It might not be fatal.'

She looked at him without speaking for a moment and Dax felt another shiver of fear. 'It's something to do with him.' She looked up towards the tower. 'And her. I feel a really strong tightness around my chest when it's her. And it's hard to breathe.'

Dax shook her hand off gently and turned away. 'Well, maybe she's an asthmatic,' he said lightly. 'But I've still got to go. Thanks, Lisa. I appreciate it.' And he hared on up the steps to catch up with Gideon.

Around the base of the chimney tower, on either side of the door, were two, high, narrow windows with thick sills. They were both ajar, and Dax could make out the voices of the principal and Caroline Fisher inside. 'Ah, Gideon,' Patrick Wood was saying. 'Have you come up to see Barber again?' Gideon made a noise of acknowledgement, clearly realizing that he had to play along, and Dax heard him move to the dog and the dog's sloppy, happy noises at the attention it was receiving, just beneath the window that Dax was crouching under. He couldn't hear or sense Mr Pengalleon in the room.

What should he do now? He needed to know that Gideon had removed the tape recorder, certainly, but this wasn't enough. He desperately wanted to see what was going on. If he were just a little smaller and nimbler he could jump up on to the thick sill and peer through the window properly. He eased up on to his toes and managed to look over the sill, catching a slice of a view of the ceiling. He jumped when, suddenly, Barber loped up on the other side of the glass, panting and snuffling around the edge of the open window. The dog looked at him and sniffed excitedly and Dax prayed he wouldn't bark. 'Shhhh!' he said, in his mind, and Barber's own mind pulse came back, 'Quiet. Fox.' Startled, Dax realized the dog really *was* communicating with him. He was even more startled, and nearly fell back down the steps, when he realized that he *was* now sitting on the sill, pushing his head round the window to meet Barber's wet sniff. And he was a fox. Dax felt the fur rise up on the back of his neck in shock. This was the first time he'd ever shifted simply because he needed to. And he'd barely even formed the *thought*.

Quickly, he pulled himself together. The principal was at the door, punching in the code and pulling it open for Caroline Fisher. 'It's your choice, of course,' he said, warmly, looking down into her face and pulsing out such a high level of glamour that even Gideon, kneeling on the floor, was watching him with his mouth slightly open and his eyes hazed over. Dax saw, to his relief, that he held his hands loosely behind his back and in them was a small, black tape recorder. Caroline Fisher was oblivious, thankfully, shaking the principal's hand.

'You've given me a lot to think about,' she said, and she seemed genuine. 'I don't want to destroy what you have here, but I need to think about what I should do.'

'Of course,' said the principal. Dax jumped down over Gideon's head, landing silently on the hearth rug, and slid under the chair nearest the door. Gideon blinked and bent down to look at him, his mouth gaping even wider now. Dax shook his head at his friend urgently, thinking 'Please! Don't react. Be still!' and both Gideon *and* Barber sat back on their haunches and carefully looked back towards the door, not making a sound.

'It's a beautiful day,' said the principal. 'Where are you parked?'

'Oh, I left my car at the hotel in the village,' said Caroline Fisher. 'I walked up this morning. It's not very far, and it's very pretty.'

'Well then, you should go back through the wood— that's even prettier,' said the principal, and Dax suddenly caught another smell that he recognized. The last time he'd noticed it was back at Bark's End Junior School, just as Clive had been skipping off with his paper clock. It had come from Matthew and Toby. Dax had known what it meant then, and he knew what it meant now. A cold feeling spread through his body.

As the door swung out wide, the principal was offering to walk Caroline Fisher through the woods and show her the path through the marsh that led around to the other end of the village. 'It's a dry path, quite safe,' he said. 'And it's lovely on a day like this.' They set off together and in the few seconds that the door took to swing back and heavily shut itself, Dax had twisted silently around the edge, flowed into the bushes that lined the driveway, and begun a silent pursuit.

He kept low and to the undergrowth. In the wood it was easy to keep them in sight, while stalking noiselessly behind the trees, fallen logs, and low vegetation. Several small creatures skittered away from him and a blackbird rose up from the bracken, chakking angrily in his path, but these were normal noises in even the quietest wood, and the principal and Caroline Fisher didn't once look back. Dax kept picking up little snatches of the same smell from the principal. But what was going to happen?

Although he didn't like Caroline Fisher and he didn't ever want to see her again, there was no way he wished any serious harm on her. But the principal *did*.

Dax had no doubt about it. Every strand and fibre of his sinewy frame and every impulse that flashed across his brain told him the same thing—*violence*—and, suddenly, inexplicably, Dax felt *responsible* for her. It was like his feeling for Alice. He had nothing in common with his objectionable little sister, but he would not stand by and see her harmed. Nor would he with Caroline Fisher. 'But what if she brings COLA Club down?' insisted a hard voice in his head. 'If he lets her go, it could be the end of Tregarren College.'

No. He'd do almost anything to save COLA Club. But not this. Whatever it was, not this.

Mr Wood wasn't carrying any weapons, as far as he could tell, but there were plenty of stout sticks and sharp branches around him. Caroline Fisher moved like a fit and healthy woman. Dax thought she'd probably put up a good fight. Maybe if he attacked the principal as a fox, he could help her in some way. He didn't feel very confident, but he trotted on, nose down and ears high, past the faint scent of the dog-fox's territory and on to the edge of the wood.

As they reached the area where the trees widened and the marshland began, Dax slowed and crouched beneath some bracken, which spread over him like a protective awning. Through gaps in the curling fronds he could see the principal slow down and turn to the reporter. Dax shifted into position, swaying his haunches in readiness to spring, his heart racing in his chest. For a while they talked, and he caught a little of the conversation. It was still calm and friendly. Dax saw the principal put his arm about her shoulders again, and steer her carefully round, pointing firmly across the marsh. He seemed to point for a very long time, and eventually Caroline Fisher nodded, and looked up at him. Dax could see the same rapt, slightly dazed look in her eyes that Gideon had had back in the gate tower. She shook his hand and he gave her a rather fatherly peck on the cheek. Beaming at him in a final glance over her shoulder, she waved once and then set out across the marsh path. And that was it.

Confused, still swaying on his haunches and still scenting violence, Dax stared through the bracken. Even now he expected the principal to suddenly give chase, but that didn't happen. He simply turned, adjusted his tie, and began to retrace his steps through the forest. He was smiling to himself and Dax heard him give a low, satisfied chuckle. But the reporter had left, freely. Once again, Dax tried to rearrange his thoughts and feelings. Was it possible that he was wrong about Patrick Wood? Had he really misjudged the man?

He glanced back at the marsh and saw Caroline Fisher walking happily across it, swinging her bag on her shoulder (she obviously hasn't checked on her tape recorder, he thought), and watching the seabirds overhead.

In his mind, Dax pictured a scene where the principal told him, 'Dax—I know I may sometimes *seem* a bit sinister, but it's really only because I have to be. I'm doing all of this to protect you and your friends. And everything's going to be fine.'

It would be so good if he could accept that. Dax longed to be able to say, 'Yes! You were right! I was really stupid, and I won't question you again, sir.'

But as the principal vanished into the trees, Dax couldn't make himself believe he ever would.

21

After a few minutes, Dax trotted out from under the bracken and headed back across the woods. He felt odd, unbalanced, as if there was something important he'd forgotten. It tickled and tickled at his brain, and he kept replaying the scene of the principal walking Caroline Fisher to the edge of the wood and seeing her off. Why did it disturb him so? He couldn't work it out, but thought that after he'd found somewhere to sleep and got back to being Dax the boy, he might.

Dax froze as the sound of fast, thudding footfalls reverberated through the woodland floor. Before he could run, he saw Gideon thundering towards him between the trees. He was closely followed by Lisa and, a little way behind, Mia. 'Dax!' panted Gideon when he saw the fox, standing uncertainly in the little clearing. 'Dax, are you OK?'

Dax nodded, although in truth he didn't feel OK. He felt as if he was staring at a puzzle, completely unable to make sense of it. And that making sense of it was deeply important.

'Lisa said you were in trouble,' said Gideon, and Dax looked up at the girl, greatly surprised.

This was the first time, as far as he knew, that she'd

approached *anyone* other than himself. She *must* be worried about him.

Lisa was glancing anxiously about her, but she paused and stared back at Dax. 'All right,' she said, 'you needn't make such a big deal about it. I just feel that I owe you one. That's all. It was Gideon that got us out—he memorized the door code.' Dax sat back on his haunches and gave her a cheeky fox grin, in spite of his worries. 'Cut it out!' she said and then resumed her searching looks through the trees.

'We saw Mr Wood come back on his own. What happened to the reporter?' asked Gideon, kneeling down next to Dax and ruffling the red fur between his ears with a look of wonder. It occurred to Dax that it was highly unlikely that Gideon would ever ruffle his *hair* like that, but he let this go. He pointed his snout in the direction he had just come from, trying to get across that she'd headed away along the marsh path.

'Which way? Point properly, with your paw or something,' said Gideon.

Then the horrible truth hit Dax like a truck.

In one, terrible, crashing moment, it all made sense. He saw again the principal walking Caroline Fisher to the edge of the wood. He saw him put his arm around her shoulder and *move* her—twist her round and *aim* her across the marsh. He saw the principal point, firmly and slowly, still holding onto the reporter, and then he saw the pulse, the wavering in the air around them.

Dax leapt to his feet as if he'd been shot at. At exactly

the same moment, Lisa gasped and fell to her knees. She wrapped her arms around her ribs and drew a strangled breath. 'Dax!' she moaned. 'Dax! You know where she *is*!' Dax began to run back to the marsh. Now Lisa cried out, 'Dax—you have to hurry! It's almost too late!'

Dax shot along the marsh path so fast that his paws made scarcely any contact with the ground. He held his snout high, scenting the air, trying to trace Caroline Fisher, but somewhere inside he already knew where she was. Dimly, he was aware of a commotion behind him as Lisa, Gideon, and Mia ran to follow him. Within seconds Dax had reached the little bridge over the nasty river of green bog and there he stopped, before turning and gazing down in the direction of the sea. He knew now that Caroline Fisher hadn't simply walked across and then somehow stumbled off the bridge. She had never even reached it. Principal Wood had clearly indicated a bridge to her and pointed her safely across to it. Only it wasn't there. Like Spook and the goalposts, Patrick Wood had simply given her mind a push and told her firmly that the bridge was some twenty metres down from where it actually was. And poor, charmed woman, she looked, and she nodded, and when she reached the bend in the path which led round to the real bridge, she had simply walked off it towards the phantom one.

Dax could smell her now. She was still on the surface, but only just. He retraced his steps to the bend in the path and, scanning across the coarse bogweed and the sinister dark patches between it, he could just make out something bright and shifting. It was a little of her blonde hair, moving in the breeze. Dax took a breath, reminding himself that he weighed only a fraction of what he did as a boy, and ran across the marsh towards her. Way behind him he heard Gideon and Mia shout, 'Dax! No! It's too dangerous!' but he felt Lisa give him a mental push. Lisa couldn't stand feeling what Caroline Fisher was feeling.

As he reached her, he saw that she was conscious but very still. All that showed of her across the stirred-up surface was one mud-caked hand, raised in a shaking curl, clearing the swamp just below the knuckles, and her face, upturned to the sky and dimmed by the brown-green slime slicked across it. Her eyes were shut tight and she seemed to be murmuring something. As Dax approached, dropping to his belly to spread his weight as evenly as possible on the thin crust of the marsh, she opened her eyes and looked at him.

'Dax,' she whispered, without surprise. 'Is that you?' Dax nodded, wondering how on earth he was going to get her out. 'It's—it's t-t-too b-bad you know,' she said, through chattering teeth, and her face gave a little, sad smile, creasing the mud that had begun to dry on it, 'I had s-so much m-more to do.' A single tear cut a pale channel through the coating on her cheek and she whispered, 'Will you t-tell my mum I'm sorry? T-tell her I love her.' Caroline Fisher closed her eyes again, as if she knew it was nearly all over.

Dax stared at her in dismay and desperation. He *couldn't* watch her drown! By now, at the bridge, he could hear Gideon and Mia shouting to him to come back; that they would run for help, but he knew there wasn't time. Inside three minutes, Caroline Fisher would be smothered. Dax leapt across at her, driving his snout down into the swamp behind her head and snatching with his teeth at the collar of her jacket. After three attempts he found it, and clenched the sodden weave in his jaws before tugging back. His hindquarters had somehow kept contact with the firmer ground and, anchored slightly, he began to pull with all his strength. The swamp pulled back, making a sighing, sucking noise as if reluctant to let go of its prey, and fury rose in the fox, a blind, primeval anger that escaped through his muddy snout as a feral shriek.

'LISA! Tell Gideon he's got to help!' Dax bawled across at her, in his head. He was aware of the girl, slumped over the guard rail of the bridge, trying to breathe, and trying to shout at Gideon. In the corner of his eye, as he tugged and tugged, and Caroline Fisher moaned as if he was disturbing her sleep, Dax saw Gideon move off the bridge and towards them, stepping quickly from clump to clump of the bogweed. Then he knelt down halfway between the bridge and Dax and Caroline and fixed his stare upon them.

For a moment there was no difference and another scream of desperation escaped from Dax's throat as he felt his front paws begin to sink into the slime, pinned down by the weight of the half-dead woman. Help me, Gideon, he pleaded in his head, *help me now*! He gave a huge tug, pulling his forepaws back out with difficulty, and shifted her by a few inches and then—and *then*—she shifted by herself. Her shoulders suddenly rose clear of the mud and then her knees emerged, glistening and thick with swamp. Dax staggered back, still holding on to her collar, as the rest of her limp body followed. Gideon was *doing it*! Dax pulled and pulled, edging back up towards the dry clumps of bogweed, and Caroline Fisher followed, half dragging, half floating, until, amazingly, Gideon was treading carefully alongside them, still steely with focus, and then they were back at the bridge.

Dax fell to his belly, panting hard. Beside him, Gideon knelt down. He was dripping with perspiration and looked dazed. Lisa was still holding her ribs and moaning, leaning against the post of the bridge, and Mia was wiping the swamp residue from around Caroline's mouth and then putting her hands down across the woman's ribs. 'Here?' she asked Lisa, urgently, and Lisa, grey and wordless, nodded.

Seeing his friends like this, in spite of his exhaustion, Dax was abruptly deluged with pure, white-hot fury. One man had caused all this. One man who thought nothing of drowning an adversary in mud while he went home for his tea. He'd been *right* about Patrick Wood all along. Dax didn't realize he was growling until three surprised faces turned to look at him. A second later, he was tearing back along the swamp path with one thought in mind: to close his sharp fox jaws around Patrick Wood's throat.

He flew through the trees, instinctively leaping

around obstacles, across ditches, over roots and logs, and found himself at the cliff edge in what seemed like seconds. Without a pause he nimbly descended the steep fox-path he had found in the moonlight, and ran swiftly between the dormitory blocks and on to the main college. He skirted the building, looking for the principal's office window, and found it open. Dax leapt onto the sill and landed on the principal's office floor with a hard clip from all four sets of claws. Patrick Wood was at his desk, indeed drinking tea and leafing through a book. He looked up in surprise, and then caution swept across his thin, uneven features.

He got to his feet, putting the cup down. 'Dax,' he said, 'what *have* you been doing?'

Dax realized that he was growling. Of course, his fur was clumped and matted together with swamp mud; it wouldn't take a genius to guess where he'd been.

Patrick Wood folded his arms and tilted his head on one side. 'Well, well,' he said, with a nasty smile. 'Been out on a little shapeshifting mission of mercy, have we?'

Dax crouched, ready to spring. The growls grew louder and wilder. The principal was emanating that scent of violence again, and it made his heart race even faster and his fury run even deeper.

Patrick Wood shrugged and strolled to the window, closing it quietly. Then he perched on the edge of his desk. 'It's a shame, Dax,' he said, as if he'd just been handed some shoddy classwork. 'Our only shapeshifter. I was looking forward to finding out what you could do;

how many different species you could be, and what use we could put you to.' Dax shifted across the room, keeping the man within springing range. Principal Wood leaned back on the desk, opening and reaching into a drawer as he continued to talk. 'Of course, what I now know is that shapeshifters aren't easy to push. Something to do with the animal instincts in you, I believe. You didn't fall for any of my little *effects*, did you, Dax? Nor did the first one.'

The first one? In a flash Dax pictured what Owen had told him. A vision of Patrick Wood kneeling beside a dead wolf.

The principal pulled something that glinted out of the drawer and sat back up on the edge of the desk, resting it in his lap.

'You see, the reason I am principal of Tregarren College is because I have what it takes to *control* people. And COLAs need control. Not by fear or threat, but by simple, honest *charm*. Well, perhaps not entirely *honest* charm. You see, nothing, Dax, *nothing* is as powerful as loyalty. There's not a COLA out there that wouldn't jump if I said so. Apart from you, of course. And your toothsome predecessor. *He* didn't like me at *all*. Animals have never taken to me.'

Dax's growl rumbled on. He didn't take his eyes off Patrick Wood for a second, but in his head and his heart he was now sick with the certainty that the principal *had* had something to do with the death of the first shapeshifter.

'Oh, you're very noble, I grant you,' Patrick Wood went on, cradling the shiny thing in his palms. 'Very decent of you to want to save poor little Caroline—but you didn't really think I was going to risk this entire college just to promote the career of some pretty little hack, did you?' he asked, and Dax growled harder. 'Be reasonable, boy. She was threatening my very existence—and yours! You should be thanking me for trying to protect you. Journalists! There are plenty of people in this country who'd like to drop the whole lot of them in a swamp.'

At this, Dax leapt. He shot through the air in a hot, blood-scented attack, and felt the principal stagger back under his jaws and claws. He was darkly thrilled to hear the man yelp with fear and to feel his clean shaven face between his teeth.

But the moment was brief. With a strong shove, Patrick Wood sent him sliding back across the floor. He cursed and raised the thing he'd been holding in his lap. 'You're just like the other one!' he hissed and pointed the gun directly at him. 'He couldn't learn to come to heel either. I just can't tolerate that.'

Dax blinked. Whatever else he'd been expecting, it hadn't been a gun—an ordinary, no-glamour gun. He froze, only his tail flicking in fury and fear.

'What do you think we're running here, Dax?' demanded Patrick Wood. 'A holiday camp? Do you honestly think it's all happy, clappy fun? Do you really think the people that run this country would allow a well-meaning *dog* to mess everything up? Oh yes—I'm able to control ninety-nine per cent of people here with my curious *talent,* but I'm just as ready to take direct action when it's necessary. That's why I'm *here.* COLAs must be controlled. Your wolfy friend learned that the hard way.'

Dax must have jumped because the principal now nodded, still training the gun on him, and pulled some SCN slips from under a glass paperweight on his desk.

'Oh yes—I know wolf-boy's been trying to get in touch,' he smirked. 'It's rather heart-warming how he wants to warn you about me. I didn't kill him, you know. He was hit by a truck. It's just that the truck driver saw a green light when there was a red one. How strange! How could such a thing have happened?' The principal's features flickered with cruel triumph as he remembered.

'Sorry, Dax,' said Patrick Wood, his concentration suddenly snapping back to the present. 'I'd like to keep you alive, but you'd be another loose cannon, like him.' He straightened his arm and squeezed the trigger and Dax looked wildly around for escape.

Just as he was about to make a dive under the desk, the door crashed open and there stood Owen.

'What's happening here?' demanded Owen but Principal Wood never shifted his gaze, or his gun, from Dax. 'Shut the door, Owen,' he said, quietly. Owen did, leaning back on it and looking from the man to the fox. Relief washed over Dax. Owen was here. He was safe.

'What's happening?' repeated Owen, not moving from the door and eyeing the gun warily.

'Our little fox friend is intent on bringing COLA Club to its knees, I'm afraid,' said the principal. 'It's not a nice job, but I'm afraid we have no choice. The future of all our children is in the balance, and we can't risk it all for the sake of one greedy shapeshifter and his friends in the press. Caroline Fisher was going to pay him a fortune for his story,' he lied. 'He duped us all, Owen. They planned it all between them.'

He moved back to the desk again, and pulled a second gun from the drawer, keeping the first levelled at Dax. 'In case I miss,' he said, handing it to Owen. 'These wild animals can move like lightning; watch him. Now remember—it has to be direct to the head.'

Now! thought Dax. Turn the gun on *him—NOW*!

But Owen didn't turn the gun on Patrick Wood. Slowly, with his face completely cold and impassive, Owen turned and pointed the gun at Dax.

2 2

For most of his life, Dax had lived with a feeling of betrayal. He never spoke of it, but it lay within him, sour and sad. First he'd lost his mother and then his father had found a replacement for her so fast that it seemed, sometimes, as if she'd never been there to begin with. And as soon as he'd got the replacement and arranged for all his son's most basic needs to be met, Robert Jones had gone, too, and stayed away as for as long as he could, preferring the cold company of the North Sea to his son. He'd left Dax to get on with it and find his own way. Bereft, and dumped in a house with Gina who didn't even like to touch him, Dax was only five when he agreed with himself to stop expecting much of people; even those who said they loved him.

If all those seven years' worth of pain and disappointment had been gathered together and loaded into a box and thrown headlong at Dax right now, it couldn't have hit him a fraction as hard as what he saw in the principal's office at that moment. Owen was betraying him. Owen.

His former friend held the gun steady for a moment, and then said in a perfectly easy voice, 'Will anyone hear the shots?' Dax began to shake with grief. He felt no fear, but the terrible truth—his complete lack of judgement over Owen—was making him faint and weak. He remembered clearly something that Owen had said to him on the evening he'd brought him to COLA Club. 'I don't set out to harm anyone,' he'd told him. 'But I know that I *could*. It's right there inside me, and it's inside you, too.' He remembered his words just an hour ago. 'There's not much I wouldn't do to protect Tregarren.'

'There's nobody at this end of the quad as far as I know,' said the principal. 'But there are plenty of easy explanations for a couple of gunshots in a place like this. Aim for his head, Owen. I know you quite like the boy, so do it quickly—it's for the best. We haven't got much time. I need to find out whether the reporter managed to get away.'

Owen flicked his colleague a glance, as if he was unaware of what had happened to Caroline Fisher.

In this moment, Dax rallied himself for one last attempt at survival. He sprang again, this time at Owen, sinking his teeth into the man's torso. The scent of him knocked Dax sideways even as Owen shoved him off. He *still* smelt like a friend. Dax yelped, far more in pain from this thought than from the rough treatment. And now Owen was moving towards him again, his face stony. He raised his gun and struck Dax hard across the snout with its barrel. Dax shot across the polished wood floor and cannoned into the bookshelves, feeling blood trickling through his fur. No! No! No! I *can't* believe it! his mind still insisted. He began to drift away, greyness rushing across his vision.

'Damn it, Hind! Don't knock him out! We need to get a shot in the head *now*. We need him to die a fox. It'll be a hell of a lot easier to get rid of him afterwards. Nobody's going to notice a dead fox at the side of the road.'

But Dax was already shifting. As his head swam with grey cloud and the blood dripped off his chin onto the floor, he realized that he was a boy again, curled up in muddy jeans, waiting to be shot by the one adult he'd trusted.

'You idiot!' cursed the principal. 'Now he's back! Wait though. I've a better idea.'

Dax opened his eyes blearily and saw Owen, crouched by him, watching his face intently. The gun rested on his knee. Dax wondered why he didn't use it. Behind Owen, he could make out Patrick Wood, pushing his desk along the floor with some difficulty.

'Come and help me, man!' he puffed and Owen, touching Dax lightly on the cheek, rose and turned towards him. Together they moved the desk off the green rug that it stood on. Then Patrick Wood pulled the carpet away and tugged a stout, metal ring out of the floor. 'Help me,' he said, again, and they hauled up a large square of its surface; a hidden trapdoor. Dax couldn't see where it led, but a musty, metallic smell rolled coldly across the floor from where the trap lay open.

Dax struggled to sit up and the principal shot him a look of triumph. 'One hundred and fifty fathoms, Dax,' he said, pointing down into the square of darkness. 'The

mine shaft. I always thought it would be useful one day.'
He stood and began to walk across to Dax, tucking his
gun into his belt. 'Come on, Owen,' he said. 'We won't
need to waste two bullets. Help me throw him down.'

Owen rose and followed the principal, and the last
shred of hope inside Dax turned to dust. He wasn't
sure it was worth fighting any more. Nothing was real.
Principal Wood could have him.

But the principal never reached him. In a swift and
sudden movement, Owen brought up his hand and
punched the man hard on the side of his head, knocking
him sideways across the room to hit the desk. Principal
Wood cried out in astonished fury and began to fumble
in his belt for the gun, but Owen already had his in his
fist and was directing it back at him. 'Leave it, Patrick,' he
said. 'Leave it *now*. You've lost. It's over!'

Patrick Wood's face turned ashen, with two high spots
of colour under his glittering dark eyes. '*Think* about it,
Owen!' he hissed. 'Once this gets out . . .'

'Once *what* gets out, Patrick? What have you *done*?
Have you killed that girl?'

'No—no, I haven't killed her,' babbled the principal,
'I just sent her over the swamp.'

'And across a bridge that wasn't there,' spat Dax, his
throat tight with both fear and joy. Owen was *not* his
enemy, after all. 'She nearly drowned, but we got her out.
She might not survive anyway.'

Owen launched himself at the principal and hit him
hard across the mouth. 'I've known you nearly ten years,'

he hissed, through gritted teeth, 'and I've always known you were manipulative and ruthless, but I *never* thought you were capable of this. It makes me sick that you thought I would help you.'

The principal seemed to slump back for a moment, but then he shoved Owen in the chest and in a moment the pair were scuffling on the floor. Owen's gun spun across to the window, unheeded, as the men struggled with each other and came perilously close to the yawning hole, still sending up its evil cold smell in the middle of the room.

'Owen! Look out!' shouted Dax, and flung himself across to grab the man and stop him hurtling down. As he did so, Principal Wood gave a howl of terror and began to slide over the edge, his hands clawing desperately for an anchor. Owen twisted on the edge too, and tried to prevent his foe from falling, in spite of everything. But when the principal shot out a last, desperate clutch for life, it wasn't Owen's wrist that he hooked on to, but Dax's ankle.

Dax was snagged and yanked down over the edge of the shaft before he could even cry out. The yells he heard came from Owen and Patrick Wood. As the rough-cut edge of the floor scrazed across his chest, Dax frenziedly scrabbled, trying to find a hand-hold, but Owen rolled over on his front and grabbed both of Dax's wrists a second before he would surely have plunged to oblivion. Then they were both jarred brutally by the full weight of Patrick Wood, who was screaming hoarsely and dangling from one of Dax's legs. Dax looked down into the inky blackness with horror. Both of the man's hands were gripped around his ankle and he was kicking and shrieking in the dead air below them. With every terrified lurch, the man jerked Dax further down into the dank shaft with him.

The pain in Dax's leg and across his chest and arms as Owen held grimly on to him was unbearable and worse with every jerk. Dax stole a last glance at his friend as he felt himself slide away. Owen's face was contorted with pain and anguish as he desperately tried to pull Dax back up, tugging hopelessly against the swinging, kicking weight of the principal. Dax closed his eyes, remembering Lisa's words to him on the cliffside steps. 'You're going to fall!' she had told him. And she'd never been wrong yet.

So this was how it ended for him. At least he didn't have to die with betrayal in his heart. He opened his eyes and gasped out, 'If you don't let go, we'll all go down.'

'*NO!*' bawled Owen, scarlet with exertion. 'No, you will *not* give up, Dax Jones!' He had hooked his feet around the legs of the heavy wooden desk, but even this was now starting to shift. Below them both, the principal swung and scrabbled and tore at the muscles in Dax's leg so hard that he thought it might actually rip off. Dax felt a wave of dizziness. He welcomed it. He'd rather not fall to his death while fully conscious.

'DAX!' Owen was yelling again. 'You've got to shift— and you've got to do it *NOW*! Do it *now*! You'll be lighter!'

The fight in him was really almost gone, and the

pain in his leg and chest was making his ears fill with a rushing-water noise, but Dax could still hear Owen calling and calling and refusing to let go, and so he gathered his exhausted spirits together and squeezed them into fox shape, one last time.

There was a terrible sound. One that neither he nor Owen would forget in their lifetime. It was the last sound that Principal Wood ever made and it was filled with the horror and fury and despair of a soul whose one chance has been lost for ever. It seemed to go on for minutes, echoing dismally back up through the well of cold, black rock, although it could only have been seconds as Owen hauled the muddy, injured fox back up on to the floor, where they both collapsed and lay staring at the ceiling.

For some minutes there was no sound but their ragged, shocked breathing, and as it gradually settled down, Dax realized that he was back in boy form again. His hip, knee, and ankle ached terribly and he could feel blood caked around the teeth on one side of his mouth where Owen had hit him with the gun. Carefully he raised his fingers to the wound and prodded it. It hurt.

Owen struggled into a sitting position. He looked pretty wrecked himself, thought Dax. His shirt was ripped at the collar and there was a nasty red welt on his cheekbone. He looked at Dax and shoved his wild hair back off his forehead. 'I'm really sorry about hitting you,' he croaked. 'I needed to get you back as a boy. I truly thought, if he saw you as a boy, and not as a fox, that he might not be able to . . . '

Dax grinned lopsidedly through his rapidly swelling mouth. 'You just saved my life. I might let you off,' he said and they both laughed, shakily and slightly hysterically, but then Dax felt his mouth pucker and he clasped his hands together to stop them shaking. 'You know he killed the other one, don't you? The one in Scotland. The wolf . . . He—I think he did a glamour on that truck driver.'

Owen stared across at the window and his bruised face creased with pain. 'I'm so sorry, Dax. I should have known. I should have known . . .'

'He said animals didn't take to him.'

Owen shook his head, awash with memory and realization of that day and this. 'The boy told him he was a fraud. Said he could smell it. He was a rough kid, you know—a street kid really. I didn't take it seriously— thought it was just his way. If I'd only . . . ' Owen bit his lip and closed his eyes.

'It wasn't your fault,' said Dax.

Owen stood up, walked to the trapdoor and dropped it back into place. It crashed shut with a billow of dust and darkness and they both shuddered. 'Come on,' he said. 'We need to get you seen to. You're a mess.'

'You've looked better yourself,' said Dax, and again, as they opened the office door, they found themselves tittering like idiots. It's the shock, thought Dax, and it was, but they still couldn't stop.

As the door closed behind them, Dax looked at Owen. 'What are we going to say to people?' he asked, subduing his giggles.

'The truth,' said Owen. 'There's no getting around it. There'll be somebody from the education department here tonight anyway. I called them myself, this morning, after Paulina Sartre and I started to get a very bad feeling about Patrick.'

Dax nodded, hoping that Owen wouldn't get into too much trouble and that people would believe what had happened. They both turned to walk carefully and painfully down the corridor towards the sanatorium, when a girl suddenly leapt out from nowhere.

Her blonde hair was flying out behind her as she aimed herself right at Owen and struck him so hard in the face that he fell against the wall. It was Lisa.

23

Dax wondered, briefly, if he was dreaming. Lisa had leapt on top of Owen and was pulling back her elbow, ready to thump him again. As she did so Owen's hand shot up and caught her wrist. 'What on earth—?' he gasped.

'Dax!' shouted Lisa, over her shoulder. 'Don't trust him! He's not on your side! He's going to shoot you and throw you down a ditch. He and Principal Wood are both in on it! I started to get it on Bonfire Night, but I didn't realize *he* was in on it until today!' She was snarling with rage and struggling furiously against Owen as he got up, holding her, with difficulty, at arm's length.

'It's all right, Lisa—he didn't shoot me! He saved my life!' shouted Dax, trying pull her off poor Owen. Lisa eased off her struggling slightly, and looked suspiciously from one to the other. She seemed to notice for the first time what a bad state they were both in.

'It's all right, really,' said Dax. 'You were right about the principal, though. And about the falling—only Owen dragged me back up again. The principal's dead,' he added, and she stared at him, dazed but not surprised. She stopped trying to kick Owen's shins, and he let go of her wrists.

'God alive, girl!' he said, rubbing his jaw. 'Where did you pick up a right hook like *that*?'

She narrowed her eyes at him for a moment, until she seemed to be satisfied that he *wasn't* about to murder Dax, and then nodded urgently up the corridor. 'Come on,' she said. 'You need to come to the san. We managed to get that reporter woman back there but she's out for the count. And it's worse than that . . . '

Before she got the chance to speak further there was a thundering of feet down the corridor and Dax was surprised to see not only Gideon but, racing ahead of him, Spook Williams. Spook didn't slow down as he reached them. He flew straight into Dax, shoving him hard up against the wall and cracking him across his tender jaw with the flat of his hand. 'Next time, you leave her *out* of it, you filthy little dingo!' snarled Spook. Dax was stunned.

'Why is everyone hitting everyone?' asked Gideon, in confusion. He had obviously just witnessed Lisa's attack on Owen. 'Should *I* be hitting anyone? Let me know. Anytime soon.' He folded his arms and waited.

'It's Mia,' explained Lisa to Dax, ignoring Spook who was actually baring his teeth at Dax now, resisting Owen's attempts to pull him off. 'I was just about to tell you. She's collapsed.'

Owen cursed and briefly shut his eyes. 'Don't tell me she tried to heal the reporter?' he groaned.

'Of course,' said Lisa, surprised. 'That's what she does.'

'Damn it, *why* didn't I stop this?' Owen raged at himself, and they all looked at him, puzzled. Even Spook released his grip on Dax and stared.

Owen started off up the corridor and they all chased after him. 'She's a brilliant healer; the best we have,' he called back to them. 'But she's way too young and she hasn't learned how to deal with the pain. I thought I'd convinced her to stop, but I didn't try hard enough.'

'What do you mean?' panted Dax, limping along behind them all.

'What do you *think* happens, when Mia takes away your pain?' shouted Owen, angrily. 'Do you think the pain bin-men come on a Friday and collect it from her? No! She keeps it all inside herself. She hasn't learned how to release it properly and she's been slowly destroying herself for the past term. And I should have stopped her!'

They all faltered a little behind him, aghast. Spook looked particularly horrified. He was clearly remembering just how bad his broken ankle had felt before Mia had healed it. Dax remembered seeing her limping slightly in Polgammon afterwards, and how tired and pale she had looked, even in the woods that afternoon. Why had he not worked it out? Why hadn't he stopped her?

When they reached the sanatorium they found it fraught with action. The two college nurses were tending to Caroline Fisher, sponging the swamp mud off her behind a screen and talking to her gently, and in a bed on the other side of the white-painted room, lay Mia. She looked as pale as the sheets and her beautiful violet eyes were huge in her face and fixed somewhere on the ceiling. She smiled vaguely as they all approached the bed, but didn't shift her gaze.

'Mia.' Owen knelt down next to the bed and took her hand. It was quite limp and cold. Mia slowly turned her face to look at him. Spook leaned anxiously on the other side of the bed and the movement made her wince and raise her other hand shakily to her ribs. Dax remembered Lisa holding her ribs, too, before and after they'd pulled Caroline Fisher from the swamp.

'Will she be OK?' said Spook, and his voice was high and tight in his throat.

'He found us carrying the reporter in,' said Lisa to Dax, quietly. 'I didn't realize Mia was in such a bad way— but she just collapsed on the cliff steps. Spook literally caught her as she fell, and carried her in here. We told him what had been happening and then he stormed off to have a go at you. Like it was *your* fault!'

'She will be OK,' said Owen.

At that moment, Mrs Sartre arrived, with three of Mia's classmates. She crossed to Owen, looking ashen. 'I think I saw something terrible,' she said, loud enough for Dax to hear. 'In the principal's study. Did I?' Owen nodded gravely and she took a breath, before lifting her head resolutely and turning back to Mia. She shooed the rest of them away, and gathered the healers round the girl. 'Take *only a little*,' she said, sternly. 'A little for each of you will be a lot from her. I will tell you when to stop.'

As the healers closed in, linking hands, Dax felt a tap on his shoulder. It was one of the nurses.

'You need sorting out,' she said and led him away. 'What happened to you?'

'Oh—well—I fell in the swamp too,' said Dax, simply. 'How is Caroline?'

'Oh, is that her name? Well, I think she'll be OK, although it looks like a couple of her ribs are broken and she's very cold and shocked. Are you her friend? Come and see her for a moment.'

She pulled a pale blue curtain aside and Dax saw Caroline Fisher lying silently on the bed. She had been bathed thoroughly and wrapped in cotton sheets and blankets like a baby. Her damp hair curled across the pillow and she opened her eyes and turned her face to look at him as he shuffled in awkwardly. She looked much, much younger. She could have been a student.

'Dax Jones.' She gave a tired smile. 'The boy who turns into a fox . . . I didn't *really* believe it, you know.'

Dax smiled back at her, ruefully. 'Not a great way for you to find out,' he said.

Gideon slid in next to him and put the small black tape recorder down on the little table beside the bed. Owen had been explaining some of what had happened in the principal's office to him and Lisa, and he was looking quite shocked. '*He* made me get it out of your bag,' he mumbled to Caroline, apologetically.

'Needn't have bothered,' she said, breathing shallowly to ease the pain in her cracked ribs, Dax guessed. 'The bag's gone to the bottom of the marsh. Don't need it anyway,' she went on, looking at Dax. 'I can't prove a thing. There's no story here. Not until you're ready to tell it, Dax.'

Dax felt a wave of relief wash over him. And then, to his immense surprise, he felt his throat close up tight and his shoulders shake. He moved quickly away from Caroline and Gideon and went to lean his forehead against the cool window at the far end of the room, watching the sea rolling gently on the horizon and feeling the novelty and the release of tears flowing down his face.

'Found some post for you, Dax!' Gideon strolled into the joint common room with an envelope and a postcard and sat on the edge of the table where Dax was reading a book on Celtic mythology (the chapter on shapeshifters) and Lisa was glumly writing out slip after slip of Spirit Communication Notices.

Dax, too, finally had some pink slips. The small sheaf which Owen had recovered from Patrick Wood's desk, all from Jessica Moorland. She *had* been about to give a message to Dax that day in the corridor, before Patrick Wood had called her aside to charm her into passing all of Dax's messages to him first. Jessica believed he was then handing them on to Dax, which, of course, he never did.

Each message read the same.

TO: *Dax Jones*
FROM: *Jessica Moorland*
The above medium/clairvoyant/audient has been contacted by spirit named: *Unsure—Wilf? Wolf?* **who wish/es you to know that:** *Stay away from the wood.*

THIS COMMUNICATION IS AUTHORIZED BY:
Mr Eades

And surely it can't have been hard for Patrick Wood to work *that* out. Not *the* wood—but Wood. Dax wondered how safe Jessica, Lisa, and the other mediums would have been if the principal had survived and *he* had fallen 150 fathoms instead.

Lisa rubbed her eyes and stretched and then muttered testily, 'All right, all *right*. Form an orderly queue! I'll get to you as soon as I can!'

'Chicken's *teeth*!' said Gideon 'How many of those have you done?'

'Seventeen, so far,' grumbled Lisa, leaning her chin in her hand. 'I've got about five months' backlog to get through. Now—pack it *in*!' She narrowed her eyes fiercely at someone they couldn't see. 'You wait till Owen teaches me to shut you out! You'll have to wait your turn then, and like it!'

Dax and Gideon laughed and Dax swiped through the air with his book, gallantly. 'Clear off!' he said. 'My friend needs a break.'

Dax read his postcard quickly. There wasn't much to read. *'Dear Dax,'* his dad had written. *'I'm really sorry I'm not going to be able to get down to see you before the end of term, but I've got two weeks off at Christmas, and I'm looking forward to hearing all about the fun you've been having.'* Dax smiled wryly to himself. *'I'll be seeing you very soon. Love, Dad.'*

The envelope was small but padded. In it Dax found

a letter, a newspaper cutting, and a small paper packet, sealed with tape. The headline on the cutting read: **BARK'S END BEAST MYSTERY SOLVED.** The story went on: **The wild animal attack on two boys at Bark's End Junior School in October occurred because a tame fox turned feral, according to police.**

The fox, which has since been destroyed, strayed into the basement of the school after its owner left a back door open. The man did not come forward for some weeks, because he did not hold a dangerous animal licence and feared he would be prosecuted.

'This only came to light after we had a call from a vet,' said Detective Inspector John Neale, from Bark's End station.

'He told us the man had brought in an elderly fox to be put down, and later confessed that it had attacked some children, and wasn't safe to keep in captivity or to be released. The parents of the children involved, and the school, have decided not to take any further action and we now consider the matter closed.'

Dax smiled and shook his head admiringly. How had she managed to cook all that up? In her letter, Caroline told him she had *'good contacts down the vet's'*. He could well imagine her using all her clever wiles to get what she wanted.

'I never got to thank you, Dax,' she wrote, *'for saving my life. I know it was Mia and Lisa and Gideon too (and please*

pass on my gratitude) but I think without you running across that swamp for me, I would never have made it. I'm only sorry that I caused you so much trouble and danger, although perhaps it's for the best that you all found out about Patrick Wood before something even worse happened.

'I hope Mia has recovered now (I know my own ribs felt ghastly for days) and that Owen hasn't had too tough a time, dealing with the authorities. The people I spoke to after I left (I had to have an official "debriefing", you know!) seemed to think very highly of him. I'm surprised that they didn't make him principal, although I hear that Mrs Sartre is a very good choice, too. Anyway, send him my regards. He's a very good man.

'But I must add, finally, that there is something that I said to you, back in the fish-and-chip cafe, that I still stand by. I don't believe you can ever completely trust the people who run COLA Club. I think most of the teachers are probably very genuine people but, Dax, I know enough about the way this country runs to tell you to be careful. Not everyone at Tregarren College is necessarily on your side—as you've already found out.

'I owe you my life, and because of that I will keep my promise not to expose you and your friends—but don't think the press and public are your only enemy.

'I hope that I turn out to be wrong about this, but in case I'm not, there's something enclosed that I want you to have. Memorize the information with it, and then carry it about you always. I hope you never need to use it, but if you do, it will always be there for you.

'Sincerely and with much affection, Caroline.'

Intrigued, Dax prised the small package open. It was

a small, ordinary house key, on a neck chain. Tucked in with it was a piece of card bearing the words, 'The Owl Box' and an address somewhere on Exmoor. Dax frowned. A cottage? A hiding place somewhere—for him to run to if he should ever have need? He was certain that it was. He read the card several times over, committing it to memory before flipping it into the open fire nearby. Then he put the chain around his neck and the key fell coolly down the inside of his sweatshirt, out of sight.

'What's that? Girlfriend sending you jewellery now?' teased Gideon.

Dax smiled. 'It's a kind of lucky charm,' he said.

'Come on, you lot,' called a voice from the door and they looked up to see Mia, warmly dressed in jeans and jumper and a thick fleece. She looked brighter and healthier than she had in weeks. They picked up their coats and followed her outside, where Lisa handed Owen her wad of pink slips. 'More to come later,' she said. She spoke wearily, but had some difficulty in keeping a small, pleased smile off her face.

Owen thanked her, with a beam. 'We'll start you on blocking in Development first thing in the morning,' he said as they headed up towards the gate tower. 'Now— everyone. Are you all ready to learn how to make a safe, efficient camp fire?'

As they threaded up into the woods it occurred to Dax that Caroline wasn't the only one preparing him for the tougher side of life. 'I'm determined that you'll all learn this before the end of term,' Owen was saying, scraping the leaf litter back to form a bare circle in the earth. 'You never know when you may need it. No matter how supernaturally charged-up you all are, you are still of this earth and you need to know how to survive on it in a crisis.'

Dax thought about the suspicions in Caroline's letter and guessed that a crisis or two was fairly likely in the years to come. He thought about the two-way mirror in B12 and the army of men in dark suits who had arrived at the college within hours and interviewed everyone in the days after Patrick Wood's death. They had all been so very *careful* with him. The other students had been told of a terrible freak accident, and although they were shocked, nobody appeared to be lastingly upset. It seemed Patrick Wood's charm was not the enduring kind.

Those that knew the truth were cautioned, gently, to say nothing—and nothing was said. The principal's body had not been recovered. There was no safe way to get 150 fathoms down to it. His office had been converted to a storeroom, the hatch nailed down, and books stacked in a pile on it. Dax had noticed that the volume which lay with its dust-jacket pressed to the hatch was Jack London's *The Call of the Wild*. The wolf boy, who had tried to warn him in dreams, had not returned, but he'd like *that*, Dax had thought, before closing the door on the new storeroom with a shiver.

The woods above the college were filled with the smells of late autumn which recharged his energy as they gathered firewood.

Gideon was flicking twigs above their heads with his hands behind his back, giggling and calling, 'Here, twiggy, twiggy! Come to be burned!' in a high, squeaky voice, while Lisa ran around, jumping up and batting them back down to him from the air. Mia was piling more on the floor and telling them off, but she was grinning and giggling too. Owen made to wade in and stop the silliness, but then for a moment, like Dax, stood back and warmly watched the fun.

Through the storm of woodland debris, he and Dax exchanged a look. We've got happiness right now, thought Dax, *here* in our hands—and instinctively he knew that Owen was thinking the same. Caroline might be right about COLA Club, but there was happiness and dismay in equal measure waiting for you anywhere in the world. Hadn't his life so far taught him that?

But with these people, thought Dax, comes my best chance. I'm *meant* to be here.

Giving his tail an optimistic wave, he leapt into the air and landed on all four paws in the middle of the sticks and the leaves and his laughing friends.

AFTER

The wolf lay on the end of his bed—he could feel its weight and warmth on his feet as he drowsed, not quite awake, not quite asleep. It was breathing gently as it turned its shaggy dark head this way and that, eyes like silver discs, reflecting the moon beyond the window.

'Are you all right, now?' Dax asked it, in his head. It nodded. 'Can you tell me about the COLAs; why we're all here?'

It looked at him, steadily, for some time. 'You're not ready to know, yet,' it told him. 'But you have a purpose. All of you.'

'But when will we know?'

'Not until after . . . '

'After what?'

' . . . you've gone to earth.'

ACKNOWLEDGEMENTS

Many thanks to: Ben McNutt, for poking about in the woods advice, Chris Packham for what it might be like to be a fox advice, and Freddy and Pauline Sparkes for the 'Why not you?' advice.

ALI SPARKES

Ali Sparkes was a journalist and BBC broadcaster until she chucked in the safe job to go dangerously freelance and try her hand at writing comedy scripts. Her first venture was as a comedy columnist on *Woman's Hour* and later on *Home Truths*. Not long after, she discovered her real love was writing children's fiction.

Ali grew up adoring adventure stories about kids who mess about in the woods and still likes to mess about in the woods herself whenever possible. She lives with her husband and two sons in Southampton, England.

HUNGRY FOR MORE?
TURN THE PAGE FOR A TASTE OF RUNNING THE RISK

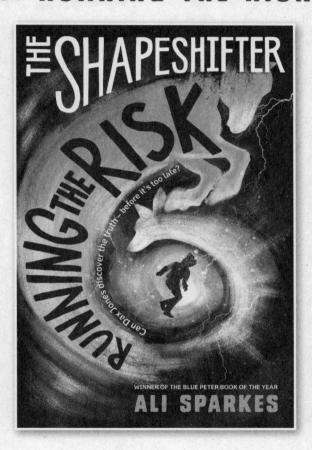

THE SHAPESHIFTER

1

The girl in grey fled across the forest—and the shapeshifter followed.

She had been running now for thirty minutes or more, and fine beads of sweat were forming on her upper lip. The creature was closing on her; she could tell. Beyond the faint chorus of birdsong she could hear only her own breathing and the thud of her expensive running shoes, but she knew without doubt that it would spring any time now. It would spring and she would be beaten. Suddenly, with a scream of surrender, she hopped up onto a fallen log and spun around to face it, hands on her hips, breathing hard. The creature leapt.

It landed softly on the log beside her without so much as a clip of its claws. It sat, curled its tail about its forepaws and regarded her with a grin which looked somewhat startling on the face of a young, red fox.

Lisa hurrumphed with annoyance. She sat down

heavily and picked some leaf litter from the instep of her running shoe. 'You have a natural advantage, Dax!' she said grumpily. The shadow of the fox flickered and curled and now Dax was checking out his own shabby trainers.

'What, with a hundred and thirty quid running shoes against these old scruffs?' he teased. 'Don't beat yourself up. You really had my lungs working this time. You're definitely getting faster.'

'Hmm.' Lisa pursed her lips and folded her arms. He hoped she wasn't going to stay in this mood. Running normally made her feel good, even when he beat her, which he always did when he was DaxFox— as DaxBoy he wouldn't have a hope. Lisa was the fittest twelve year old he'd ever met.

'What's up?' he asked, knowing he probably wouldn't
get an answer.

'Nothing,' she muttered, getting to her feet.

'More messages?' Dax peered at his friend. A wellturned-out blonde (babe in waiting, was what Gideon called her), she didn't look the type to be bothered by more than where her next new outfit was coming from, but, sadly, Lisa had had more to be bothered by in the past twelve months than most people get in a lifetime.

'Nothing!' she said, with that warning note in her voice.

'Come on—let's run back to the others now,' said Dax. 'I won't shift this time—so it'll be fair.'

She glanced at him. 'You're just humouring me!' she said, but with a flicker of interest. Lisa loved winning.

'Yep!' agreed Dax. 'But you've got to give me a head start!' He bounded off the log and away back through the trees and Lisa gave him precisely five seconds before giving chase. She passed ten seconds later. Good. He hoped the extra sprint might do the trick for her. When the messages came they could sometimes be very dark and unpleasant. Often they came with visions. Not that you'd ever know with Lisa. There was no airy-fairy stuff about the girl; no spooky voice and fluttering eyelids.

When Lisa got a trance the most you'd be likely to notice was a slight rubbing of her left shoulder while she stared hard at something. Sometimes she got a cold patch of pins and needles there. 'Like they're leaning on it, yakking in my ear!' she'd complained once.

Frankly, Lisa did not hold with the spirit world communicating with the earthly one—especially when the spirits chose to communicate through her, which they'd been pretty much queuing up to do since last summer. There was no question that her unwelcome gift was a useful one, though. Lisa could find lost things in a matter of seconds. You only had to ask and she'd raise her eyes to the heavens and mutter at you, close them briefly for a second, and then tell you exactly where your missing sock or key or bar of chocolate was. Sometimes she'd get fed up and say testily, 'Don't be so lazy. Have a look before you ask me!' She always knew when they hadn't.

Finding lost people was the less pleasant part of her ability. Usually they were dead lost people, or worse, people who were lined up for being dead fairly soon.

When he finally caught up with her, she was back with Gideon and Mia in the clearing. Gideon was still lying on the grass, half asleep in the warm spring sun, his freckled arm covering his eyes, a ladybird settled on his tufty fair hair, and Mia was sitting up, her arms around her knees, peering at Lisa closely. Going by Mia's expression, the extra sprint hadn't helped Lisa much. Lisa was flopped down on her knees, dragging the scrunchy band out of her hair and shaking her ponytail loose with a growl of frustration. 'Eeeesh! I hate these ones!' she cursed. She worked her fingers rapidly across her scalp and then down onto her left shoulder, as best she could reach. Mia moved across to her and touched her head gently with one hand. Within a second Lisa's face softened and the stressed lines across her brow eased away. Even two metres away, Dax could feel the soft cool pulse of Mia's healing.

'She all right?' he panted, skidding to his knees next to the two girls.

'She's fine,' muttered Lisa, grumpily, but not with much aggression. 'It's just this wifty-wafty, faffy, fluffy, blitblat . . . ' she tailed off, but they all got it. The thing Lisa hated most about her ability was the vague bit; the sense of something about to happen, but no firm idea of what.

'Is it one of us?' asked Mia.

'Yes—no—I don't know!'

'Well, stop grinding your perfect little teeth—you know it won't help!' said Gideon from under his arm. 'The more manic you get about it the harder it'll be to work it out!'

Lisa's eyes flashed and Dax thought serious trouble was brewing for Gideon.

HAVE YOU READ
THEM ALL?

THE SHAPESHIFTER